A TAIL OF TWO SQUIRRELS

A WILDWOOD WITCH MYSTERY: BOOK NINE

ELLE ADAMS

1

"Hello again, Robin Wildwood."

Linnea's wide smile was betrayed by the coldness in her eyes as we stared one another out. The Reaper and the Head Witch. Or rather, the former Reaper who'd gained her title by murdering her own boss and the barely qualified Head Witch who'd gained her own position due to being chosen by an inanimate stick. Technicalities.

Though Linnea didn't exactly look the part of an ex-Reaper who'd just broken out of jail with the aid of an army of monsters. She was a short woman with pale skin and a cloud of black hair. She wore her usual petite black dress, and the only hint of the power she possessed was the shadowy haze around her body that made her look as if someone had outlined her in Sharpie.

"Not going to reply?" she said to me. "I thought you'd have something to say. You usually do."

I peeled my tongue from the roof of my mouth. "I have a few things to say, but nothing suitable for polite company."

She gave a laugh. "Still playing the coven's games, are you, Robin?"

Her gaze panned over my equally silent companions. Even my mother, who always held it together in a crisis, and my usually uptight brother—the head of law enforcement—were rendered speechless. So were the Wardens, who'd been called to investigate a jailbreak at one of their high-security prisons just a few minutes earlier only to find the person who'd broken out of jail had come straight here to Wildwood Heath.

Tansy, my squirrel familiar, broke the silence with a stream of expletives. Unfortunately, since nobody outside my family could understand a word she said, Linnea likely heard nothing but squeaking, which kind of ruined the effect a little.

"No, and I'm not playing *your* games, either," I said to Linnea. "When you tag-team with man-eating monsters from the afterworld to intimidate me, you don't deserve a minute of my attention. Now get out of my town."

"I don't think so." She gave me a flat stare. "I have a job to do here."

That can't be good.

The last time we'd met face-to-face, I'd had no idea Linnea's mother had been killed by the same demons who'd developed a powerful grudge against my family after my grandmother banished them to the depths of the afterworld. Why she blamed *me* for that was as much a mystery as why she'd seemingly allied with those very demons herself.

"Does that job involve those demons?" I asked. "The ones that killed your family?"

Her mouth twisted, no longer smiling. "You have no idea what you're talking about."

"I know the truth, Linnea." Out of the corner of my eye, I saw the others reaching for their wands, and I raised my voice to keep Linnea's attention on my face. "I know what really happened all those years ago."

"Do you now?" she said. "I highly doubt it."

"Everyone knows," I went on. "My aunt is in jail because of her role in your family's deaths. I'm the one who got her arrested for it. I'm not your enemy."

She laughed again, this time without any humour. "This is all the fault of your family, Robin. It's too late to turn back."

"My grandmother *banished* the demons," I pointed out. "She saved everyone. I'm sorry she didn't get there in time to stop them from killing your mother, but—"

But your mother summoned the demon in the first place.

I didn't say that part out loud, but from the tightening of her jaw, I could tell she'd heard my unspoken words all the same. It was hard *not* to mention it, given that summoning a demon on purpose wasn't the sort of mistake one typically walked away from unscathed. Regardless, Grandma was hardly at fault, not compared to my Aunt Shannon. She was the one who locked Linnea's mother and her coven inside a house with the demons—the ones they'd summoned—when she discovered her husband was having an affair with one of said coven members.

And to think *I* was supposed to be the family screwup.

Linnea surveyed me through narrowed eyes. "I wouldn't push me, Robin."

"Or what?"

She was outnumbered—or so it seemed. In addition to my mother and Ramsey, Perry and Farley were witches, Maurice was a vampire, Callum was a werewolf, and I wasn't entirely sure what Tam was, to be honest. But none of them had a Reaper's skills, and my only Reaper contact was on the other side of the country.

"Or else I'll have to call my friends."

The darkness outlining her body thickened, and as the

shadows expanded, shapes began to emerge—giant shaggy monsters as dark as the blackness from which they appeared. Ghasts, perhaps the same ones my family and I had trapped in the forest earlier that day, were now free to obey her command. Two emerged, then four, then six, fanning out behind her into a threatening line.

Oh boy.

Not only were the ghasts a considerable threat on their own, but the two demons we'd recently banished weren't deep enough into the afterworld to stop a Reaper like her from calling them back with ease.

The knowing smile on her face told me that precise thought was on her mind. "Last chance to surrender," she said. "If you and your family members come with me quietly, Robin, I'll leave the rest of your town alone."

"A likely story," I said.

I kept an eye on my mother—Linnea would pick her out as the obvious weak link, given her recent awakening from a coma caused by a stint in the afterworld, courtesy of Linnea herself. Not that anyone else in the coven was in great shape either. Linnea had trapped everyone inside the coven head-quarters—where they remained—including all the council members and my assistant, Chloe. With my Aunt Shannon on her way to jail—deserved though it might be—we lacked firepower, to say the least.

Time to improvise.

I lifted the sceptre and cast a freeze-frame spell. Though Linnea didn't so much as twitch, darkness swept over her body like a shield, and my spell bounced clean off her.

My family leapt into action as the ghasts closed in around us. My mother and brother lifted their wands, as did Perry and Farley, while Callum shifted into his wolf form and ran to confront the monsters alongside Maurice, his vampire teammate. Together, they drove two of the ghasts into retreat while Tam engaged a third with a pair of sticks that he wielded with expert precision. Whatever kind of paranormal he was, he moved fast enough that the ghasts couldn't land a hit on him.

Linnea stood amid the chaos with a knowing smile on her face as she watched the ghasts advance on my family. My freeze-frame spell hit two of the monsters and turned them into monster-shaped statues, but a third ghast leapt at my brother, claws outstretched. My mother waved her wand and sent the beast flying head over heels. Exhaustion lined her face, and I felt a prickle of alarm. She'd barely survived her last encounter with Linnea, and she was in no shape to weather another attack.

As I ran to my mother's side, two more ghasts appeared. I reached into my pocket and pulled out a handful of sage, then I waved the sceptre in the motion for a levitation spell to guide the sage into a circle on the ground. I couldn't banish every creature at once, but one or two at a time would be doable, and a circle of sage was an effective measure to keep them contained.

In a sweep of the sceptre, I sent the two newcomers flying back into the sage circle and cast a banishing spell.

Hot breath seared my neck. Another ghast had appeared at my back, teeth bared, ready for the kill.

The sceptre ignited. Purple light flared, blasting the creature full in the face, and another sweep of the instrument sent the monster stumbling into the sage circle. As I readied myself to cast the banishing spell for a second time, Linnea laughed.

"Impressive, Robin… but too late. Look."

I couldn't help myself. I looked—at Linnea and the dozen or more ghasts that now surrounded the coven headquarters.

The people inside couldn't defend themselves. Thanks to Linnea, they were trapped, completely at her mercy.

"Stop that at once!" My mother ran towards them, lifting her wand.

What is she doing?

"Mum!" I began to run, too, but one of the ghasts had already lifted a claw to strike her.

"Get *out!*" The scream came from inside the building, loud enough to make my eardrums burn.

Grandma's ghost popped up in a whirlwind that sent me staggering sideways, off balance. All the ghasts retreated, pushed back from the witches' headquarters and from my mother, and two of the monsters vanished outright. A third, too, fled into the afterworld. My mother was also knocked sideways but recovered quickly, getting swiftly out of the way of the oncoming claw.

The only person unaffected was Linnea, whose eyes narrowed. "You."

With her attention fixed on Grandma, I moved closer to my mother and whispered, "You can't take them on alone."

Perry limped over, her hair plastered to her face with sweat. "None of us can. We're surrounded."

The other Wardens were in a bad way too. Farley was on her knees, her hands over her head, while Callum lay on his side, groaning, back in his human form again. Maurice stood defensively in front of them, but even the vampire appeared small when faced with the two giant oncoming shaggy monsters. Two more had Tam engaged in a deadly dance, and though the Wardens' leader was swift on his feet and adept with those stick-like weapons, how long would he last if Linnea kept summoning more monsters to take the place of each one he brought down?

"Tam says we have to get out," Perry said in an undertone. "But we'll have to go through the forest."

"What?" My heart sank. "We can't leave. We live here. Also, the forest is where those monsters are coming from."

"The town is bound," she said. "Transportation spells can't be used. I tried."

My heart plunged even further. "She put another shielding spell around the forest?"

I'd used a similar spell myself to prevent anyone with bad intentions from getting into the town, except when applied in reverse, this spell meant none of us could get *out* of the town. Calling for backup from outside was out of the question. They'd arrive too late.

Linnea, by contrast, could use the afterworld to step from one place to another with ease—no matter how far apart. Nowhere was out-of-bounds for a Reaper.

"Give it up, Robin," Linnea called. "I don't want to harm the people of this town. If you surrender, I won't harm another soul."

"I'll die first."

I'd gladly trade my life for those of my family members and friends, but I didn't believe for a minute that complying with her requests would win my loved ones anything other than a tiny bit of time before she changed her mind and killed them all anyway. Linnea was unpredictable as hell, with a grudge as deep as the darkest corner of the afterworld. Moreover, I was Head Witch. It was my job to defend the people of Wildwood Heath against people like her.

And yet—I couldn't protect them all. That was the truth of the matter, an insidious voice whispered in the back of my mind no matter how I tried to suppress it.

The sceptre can't beat her. If I keep fighting, my family will die.

"We can run into the forest," Perry murmured in my ear. "You know it better than she does, don't you?"

I did, and the forest would also be an ideal way to lure those monsters of hers away from the town. Whether leaving was cowardly or not, I'd never forgive myself if innocent people paid the price for Linnea's grudge.

Dammit.

Perry was already backing away, an apology in her eyes. "I'm sorry, Robin, but Tam said there'll be backup waiting on the other side of the forest. It's the only way we'll get out of this alive."

A warning growl came from the ghasts, which had begun to shake off the effects of Grandma's shout. It was now or never.

I leaned closer to Mum and whispered, "The Wardens are going to try to lure the monsters away. The town's boundaries are locked, so we can't use transportation spells."

"Out of the question—" Mum's reply was cut off when one of the beasts swiped at her, knocking her flat onto her back.

"Hey!" I retaliated with a knockback spell that sent the beast flying into the path of Perry's wand. As it froze into a block of ice, Ramsey ran to help Mum to her feet.

I moved to his side and hissed, "The Wardens have backup on the other side of the forest. We're the ones she wants dead. If we lure the monsters away, they'll leave the town alone."

"I…" Ramsey's weary gaze went to Mum, who staggered against him, hardly able to stay on her feet. "You'd better be right."

"I'll distract her," I added. "You get Mum out of here."

Mum leaned on Ramsey, her breathing shallow. Neither argued. They followed Perry's lead while I ran towards Linnea and raised my sceptre to the sky.

"Come and get me!" I shouted.

Then I ran full tilt past her, casting a flight spell as I did. My feet left the ground in an inelegant swoop that would have made a Sky Hopper player cringe to watch, but since I hadn't used a transportation spell, Linnea's shield had no effect on me.

I took off like a rocket and flew in a lopsided circuit that kept Linnea's attention off Mum and Ramsey long enough for them to reach the forest path safely. Once I was sure they were out of Linnea's line of sight, I flew at the mass of trees marking the boundary between the Wildwood and the road.

I picked up speed, pursued by Linnea's scream of rage and the growls of rampaging ghasts plunging into the woods after me. I'd deliberately aimed in the direction opposite the path Mum and Ramsey had taken and flew in a wild zigzag motion that caused the ghasts to swiftly find themselves tangled in thorns and briars. My own cloak kept snagging on branches, too, but I continued to weave amid the trees like an amateur flier caught in a storm.

Then, in similar fashion, I crashed straight into a tree.

Birds flew around my head—literally, as I'd disturbed a nest—and I rubbed my forehead dizzily, trying to figure out where I'd landed. Then I spied a red blot with a fluffy tail making its stealthy way through the trees too. *Tansy.*

"She's behind me!" she squeaked, pointing with her tail. "So is your brother."

My heart plummeted. I could see Ramsey nearby, running as fast as he could while supporting my mother, but a ghast was swift on their heels. Behind walked Linnea, her gaze roving over the treetops—searching for me.

"Leave them alone!" I leapt out of the tree, casting a spell as I fell. The ghast was sent flying back into its summoner, who vanished in a swirl of shadow.

Another sweep of my wand broke my fall. My knees buckled on landing, and I looked up to see Linnea stepping out from behind a tree, unhurt.

"Running away, are you?" she asked.

"No, running for help. Did you forget you angered all the local Wardens when you pulled off your jailbreak?"

"Now, I did tell you that I'll avoid harming the citizens of the town if you cooperate, didn't I?"

"I don't think so."

I launched into a sprint—the best I could with branches, leaves, and panicking birds blocking my path. Ordinarily, I'd have used my magic and commanded the birds to attack Linnea, but most animals were terrified of the dead. Tansy was certainly no exception. She ran across the treetops, her paws skimming the branches so rapidly she might as well have been flying.

I flung a freeze-frame spell over my shoulder, my arms screaming from the effort of holding the sceptre up as I ran. As my route steepened, I overtook the Wardens, who had been slowed by their injured teammates, and burst out of the trees onto the hillside.

Gasping for breath, I braced my hands on my knees. Behind me, the Wardens emerged with Tam in the lead.

"I thought," I wheezed, "you called for backup."

"I did." Tam raised his stick-like weapons in both hands as the shadow of a ghast appeared amid the trees, then a second one.

Mum and Ramsey came staggering out first, with the two ghasts fast on their heels. I pointed my sceptre at them and cast a freeze-frame spell, wondering where in hell the rest of the Wardens were.

"Where's your backup?" Linnea sidled out of the trees, behind her monsters. "You really should have made sure they weren't already occupied."

Perry's eyes widened. "What have you done?"

"I *may* have caused a little diversion at the jail when I escaped."

There's no backup.

Half of us were injured, more than a dozen ghasts were on our tail, and if the shadows growing around Linnea were any indication, she was gearing up to summon far worse. Like those demons.

"I told you to give up, Robin." She lifted a hand to point to my mother. "I think I'll finish her off first."

I threw the sceptre into the air.

It was not my best idea—I freely admit that, but the sceptre's vibrant glow distracted the monsters and drew Linnea's eye too. In that heartbeat of her hesitation, I ran in front, placing myself between her and my family. The sceptre tumbled in midair, and as I caught the end between my fingertips, I turned the motion into a transportation spell.

Everything seemed to slow down.

As Wildwood Heath began to fade, Linnea flickered out of sight and reappeared at my back, her fingers closing over the sceptre. She screamed as if in pain, and I shook it, trying to break her grip.

In another heartbeat, we were swept away—the town vanished and, in the same instant, was replaced by a hillside. My knees buckled as the world tilted sideways, my brain trying to adjust to the sudden change of scenery.

A groan pointed me to Ramsey, who was flat on his back next to my mother with Tansy sitting on his chest. A loud *thump* sounded nearby, followed by a series of growls, thuds, and animal noises. Alarmed, I moved that way and found the Wardens had had an equally rough landing and seemed to have brought one of the ghasts along for the ride.

Luckily, the ghast was equally disorientated. With the practised ease of those used to fighting monsters, Maurice and Tam soon had the beast pinned down. Perry and Farley moved in with their wands raised to cast a banishment spell, and the chorus of snarls dissipated as the beast vanished back into the darkness from which it had come.

Perry turned to me with a sheepish look on her face. "Sorry. I'm really bad at transportation spells, and I think you and I cast them at the same time. I don't know where we are, to be honest."

"Nor me." I rubbed my forehead and looked for the others. "Mum? Ramsey?"

Both were on their feet, staring at me—or more specifically, at my hands and at the object that should have been there but very much wasn't.

I scanned the hillside, searching for a spark, a glimmer of purple light. Nothing.

We'd escaped… but I'd lost the sceptre.

2

The sceptre.

Did Linnea take it?

No, it'd hurt her hand when she touched it. I'd seen her face, twisted into a grimace of pain.

I ran downhill, eyes open for any signs of the long, pointed instrument. The sceptre's glowing purple gem was distinctive even as far as magical objects went, but I didn't see so much as a glint between the top of the hill and the river near the bottom that I belatedly recognised as the one that ran through Yarrowfield, the town in which I'd lived for a few years prior to being dragged back to my family's home.

"Robin!" Ramsey called. "Where are you going?"

"I know where we are." I jogged back up the hill, my heart sinking when I saw Mum lying limply on the grass, her eyes closed. I crouched beside her and lifted her wrist, relieved to feel a pulse, albeit a faint one.

"Overexerted herself." Ramsey looked pale and tired himself. "We can't stay out here. We're exposed."

"We're near my old flat," I told him. "We can take Mum

there for now. It's not far, and Linnea doesn't know where I used to live."

My brother's mouth pressed into a line. Then he jerked his head in a nod. "I'll take her."

He flicked his wand to levitate Mum's unconscious body into the air. I watched with a distinct sense of unreality at just how quickly things had gone so wrong. I'd lost the sceptre. I should be running back to Wildwood Heath to get it, to fight Linnea, but it also felt viscerally wrong to abandon Mum at a time like this.

And the rest of my family? My friends? Worry reared inside me as I thought of all the people Linnea might target in our absence. But if I returned now, I might be condemning them all.

"Are you all right?" Perry walked over to us. "Tam's trying to get through to the jail, but nobody's picking up the phone."

"Oh no."

At least everyone in Perry's team was back on their feet, though Farley looked a little unsteady. Callum, who'd left his clothes behind when he'd shifted into wolf form, was draped in what looked like a curtain, presumably conjured up by one of the others. Maurice paced around them, looking furious.

Tam approached with a phone in his hand. "The lines are busy. We'll have to go there in person."

"Hope that means they're busy recapturing everyone Linnea set free on her way out," Perry remarked. "Robin— where's the sceptre?"

"Gone." My voice sounded small. "I don't know where I dropped it."

"On the hillside near the forest," said Tam. "I saw it fall from your hand as we were disappearing, but we moved too fast to grab it."

He must have sharp vision to have picked up on that. I sure as hell hadn't. "I have to go back."

"And your family?" Tam gestured to Ramsey, who was making his way downhill with Mum bobbing awkwardly alongside him. "Where are they going?"

"My old flat is near here. My brother's taking Mum there for the time being since Linnea doesn't have that address."

Not that that would stop her from searching—as a Reaper, she had free run of both the physical and spirit worlds.

What choice do I have, though?

We were far outgunned, and even the Wardens were ready to leave.

Perry gave me an apologetic look. "I wish we could come with you, but we have to go see what kind of chaos Linnea caused at the jail when she escaped."

I understood, given that there had been other criminals locked in there. Dangerous ones. "I know."

"But we'll come back," she added. "We can set up some shielding spells surrounding your flat in case Linnea sends more of her monsters after you."

That sounded like she thought we'd be staying for the long haul. It wasn't the worst plan—Linnea had no idea where I'd lived prior to my return to Wildwood Heath, and Mum needed somewhere to recover—but guilt over the people I'd left behind gnawed at me all the same.

I gave Perry my address then followed my brother downhill into the village of Yarrowfield, a settlement so small and unremarkable that it made Wildwood Heath look like a thriving city by comparison. One perk of its small population was that we attracted few stares when my brother levitated Mum down the street and into the three-storey block where I'd once lived. As I'd paid to the end of my lease and had access to the building for the next six months or so, it was unlikely the landlord would come bursting in—or so I hoped.

The flat itself contained little furniture aside from an old sofa and two armchairs. We laid Mum on the sofa and each claimed an armchair, though neither of us sat down. I couldn't settle, and neither could Ramsey. A muscle ticked in his jaw as he pulled out his phone, his other hand running through his unusually tangled blond hair.

I checked my phone too. No messages yet. Dad might not even have noticed anything was wrong… or Linnea might have already found him.

Calm down. She doesn't know you're related.

Dad wasn't the only potential target if Linnea decided to go after those close to me—like my boyfriend, Harvey, my best friend, Piper, or my cousin Rowan, who'd be working at the café, oblivious to the danger loose in town.

I sucked in a breath and typed a message to Dad first, warning him not to leave the house. We'd already set up anti-demon defences around his cottage, but it wouldn't take much effort for Linnea to remove them.

"Don't send any messages," Ramsey warned. "What if she's tracking us?"

"She doesn't need to tap my phone to do that," I replied. "Don't forget there's no place on earth off-limits to a Reaper."

Which suggested the first person I should call was a Reaper of my own, but Linnea might well give Maura a run for her money, and I didn't need to think too hard to imagine the objections my brother would have if I suggested calling her in to help us. Hadn't all this started because I'd put my trust in Linnea, assuming a Reaper would never break the rules and join forces with the same monsters they were supposed to banish?

"I'm warning Dad." I sent the message. "I need to do the same to Rowan and Harvey before they decide to fight back. I don't want them to get hurt."

"I'll go back," he said. "I'll check on them after I send my team to capture Linnea and her monsters."

"Are you sure that's a good idea?" I asked. "Those monsters of hers outnumbered the entire police force—easily—and that's assuming she hasn't brought in anyone new."

"What else am I to do?" he retaliated. "Fight them alone? Or let you do it, without the sceptre?"

That was a low blow.

"I'll get it back. Nobody else can use it, including Linnea."

It had been the sceptre that had chosen me for the role as Head Witch in the first place, and more recently, it had also rechosen me when my scheming Aunt Shannon had tried to snag the position for herself.

"Spy!" Tansy leapt overhead, her fluffy tail wagging, and vanished behind the sofa.

I watched, bewildered, as a scuffling noise ensued, followed by a series of yelps. Then Tansy emerged—no, a *second* red squirrel did, pursued by Tansy herself. In another flying leap, she had the intruder pinned down. The second squirrel was a little smaller than Tansy, and given their rarity in the wild, I was willing to bet that I knew exactly who it was.

"What are *you* doing here?" I demanded. "Come to spy on us? Did Linnea send you?"

"No!" Radcliffe the squirrel said indignantly. "I came to help you."

"A likely story," I said. "You worked for the enemy once before. Why would I believe you've had a change of heart?"

"I've never worked for the rogue Reaper!" he squeaked. "Never!"

That was true, admittedly, though the last person he'd spied on me for was hardly trustworthy either. Why would he switch to my side at a time like this? And why would he be hiding inside my old flat?

"Did you follow us here?" I asked. "Tell me the truth."

Tansy held him pinned down. "Answer her."

"I was in Wildwood Heath," he squeaked. "I saw Linnea in the forest and came to warn you, but everything happened so fast."

"I don't believe you," said Tansy. "Want me to toss him out the window?"

"Tansy, ease up. I want to ask him some questions." I narrowed my eyes at the other squirrel. "Give me more details. Where exactly did you see Linnea? What did she do?"

"I saw her cast a spell to remove the sage circles you trapped those monsters in," he replied. "I was going to come and warn you, but they moved too fast, and so did she."

My phone buzzed. I jumped, recognising the number as Dad's. His message said everyone was safely at home but that he'd heard some strange noises in the forest. I replied, telling him not to leave the house until I said so. As I hit send, another text came in from Piper, asking what was going on. I typed a hurried reply, my heart racing.

"I can go back to Wildwood Heath and check on anyone you want me to," Radcliffe offered. "I'm good at sneaking around without anyone knowing I'm there."

Dammit.

Was this an attempt at manipulation? If it was, I couldn't see what the squirrel could possibly hope to gain from helping a Reaper hellbent on summoning monsters that struck terror into the heart of any creature, human or otherwise.

"If anyone is going to spy on her, it'll be me," Tansy insisted. "And *I'll* help our friends."

"It's too dangerous." Radcliffe might not be fully trustworthy, but at least he wasn't on Linnea's list of targets. Though she might mistake him for Tansy anyway. *Hmm.*

Another message came in, this one from Rowan. My eyes raced down the screen, the words tangling themselves into illegibility before I made sense out of them. "Rowan said Linnea is marching through the middle of town with those monsters of hers. Not sure where she's going."

My mouth went dry. I hadn't heard from Harvey yet, nor Piper, either.

What is Linnea doing?

Ramsey swore, startling me. His eyes, too, were fixed on his phone screen. "Seth says Linnea came into the police station. I have to go back."

I grabbed his sleeve, indicating Mum. "You said we can't leave her behind. What's Linnea doing at the jail?"

"I'll help!" Radcliffe insisted. "I look just like your familiar, don't I? I can divert her attention while your allies get out."

My mouth parted. The same thought had crossed my mind, but I was surprised he'd volunteer for such a dangerous job.

"Don't fall for it!" Tansy said. "He means to betray us. He'll tell Linnea where we're hiding."

He might, but there was a high chance Linnea would soon work it out regardless. If he was serious about helping, leading Linnea astray might win enough time for Dad and the others to get out.

"Look, he's not that dangerous," I told her. "If he does decide to help Linnea, it's not going to give her much more of an advantage than she already has."

"I won't!" Radcliffe squirmed away from Tansy's claws. "Please, let me help you. I want to make up for my mistakes."

"A likely story," said Tansy.

Did I trust the squirrel? Not remotely. But the worst that could come of involving him was that he'd chicken out and run for the hills. He wasn't of any use to Linnea. A Reaper had no need of a familiar to spy on us when the entire afterworld was at her beck and call.

Mum groaned, stirring on the sofa. "What is going on?"

"Don't stand up," my brother warned. "You're exhausted. You need to rest."

"Where am I?" She blinked then lifted her head to glance around the room.

"My old flat," I told her. "Linnea had us on the run. She doesn't know we're here."

Her gaze passed over the threadbare furniture, the stained wallpaper, the worn carpets. "You lived here? In this... *hovel?*"

My eye twitched. Typical that she found the energy to be judgemental even in her current state. "This is the only place I could think of to hide until the Wardens get backup."

Whenever *that* was.

Mum tried to stand but fell back onto the sofa.

Ramsey leaned over her, concerned. "Take it easy."

"I'm fine." She looked at Tansy then Radcliffe. "Why are there two squirrels?"

If I'd been feeling vindictive, I might have said there was just one and that she was seeing double—just to make her take her own health seriously. But that would be mean. "The other one's offering to go back to Wildwood Heath to check on the others."

"You mean the council?"

Oops. I'd completely forgotten the council members, who'd been left trapped inside their own headquarters alongside my assistant, Chloe. "I meant Dad and his family. Anyone she might use as leverage against me."

"She's at the police station," said Ramsey, looking at his phone. "Seth locked himself in my office. He says she went into the jail, probably to talk to anyone willing to help her."

My heart dropped. "Like Tiffany Henbane."

"And my sister."

My head whipped to Mum, surprised. "You think Aunt Shannon will help Linnea?"

"I certainly think she'll try to take advantage of the situation to get herself out of jail, if she can," she said. "And we all know she'll go to any lengths to further her own ambitions."

"I know that, but she and Linnea didn't exactly hit it off." Sudden horror rose inside me. "But if Linnea goes looking for people to use as bait to lure me back into town, I bet Aunt Shannon would sell out my dad and his family in a heartbeat."

"She's right," Ramsey said. "I wouldn't be surprised if she saw a way to make herself invaluable to Linnea *and* to hit back at our family for getting her arrested."

Mum's jaw tensed. She and Dad had had a rocky history, to say the least, and in a crisis like this, her own immediate family would always come first. I watched her, heart in my throat. If she told me to leave them behind…

"No," she said. "We need to get them out of there."

3

I stared at my mother in surprise. She and I rarely agreed on anything, especially concerning my father and his family. Mum had disapproved of pretty much all my dad's life choices after their divorce, including his decision to marry a shifter and take on a parenting role for the two kids Jessica already had. Even Ramsey had only recently taken steps towards reconciliation with that side of the family, having irrationally blamed our parents' separation entirely on Dad.

My phone buzzed again. I saw Harvey's number and nearly dropped it, catching the phone in trembling fingers. "Harvey's okay. He said he's going—oh no."

"What?" said Ramsey.

I frantically typed a reply. "He said he's going to confront her. Linnea. I'm telling him to help Dad instead. He has a broomstick, so he can get around the shielding spell Linnea put on the town."

"Good point." Ramsey's expression cleared then clouded. "He can't carry our father's entire family, though."

"Jessica and the kids can shift," I reminded him. "They can

outrun those monsters if they have a head start while Dad hitches a ride with Harvey."

Of course, first we needed to give Dad and the others that head start. I swivelled to Radcliffe. Tansy had finally climbed off him, though she watched him suspiciously with her tail twitching in a manner she usually reserved for any local grey squirrels who encroached on her territory.

Harvey's reply came quickly and brought a sigh of relief. "Harvey will help Dad and his family get out. If Linnea's still at the jail, this might be our only shot to smuggle them out of town before she realises."

"I can distract her!" Radcliffe squeaked. "Just give me the word."

I took in a breath. "I swear—if you're planning to double-cross us, I'll make you sorry."

"I don't trust him a bit," Tansy announced. "*I'll* distract her."

I tuned out their argument as a reply from Rowan came in next saying that Linnea had yet to emerge from the jail. Both Rowan and Piper were potential targets, but Rowan had it worse since she was related to me *and* to Aunt Shannon. I sent a message urging her to leave with Harvey and the others, hoping Piper would evade Linnea's notice. She was only the family's gardener, not privy to the coven's secrets.

Then again, I wasn't sure that Linnea even cared about the coven. She'd trapped everyone on the council inside the headquarters and left them there, and as far as I knew, she hadn't even tried to ransack my office. Maybe Grandma had chased her off.

Grandma. I didn't like leaving her in the same town as a cantankerous Reaper, but smuggling *her* out of Wildwood Heath would have been out of the question, even if she didn't outright refuse.

I slid my phone into my pocket and turned to address the squirrels. "Stop arguing. Neither of you is going to distract Linnea—not until I say so."

"I'll do it," Tansy insisted. "I'll grab the sceptre while I'm at it and turn her into a bat."

"The sceptre." Mum looked sharply at me. "Where is the sceptre?"

Uh-oh. "Linnea grabbed me while I was casting the transportation spell to get us out, and I must have dropped it."

I held my breath as Mum studied me for a heartbeat. Strangely enough, the absence of any obvious emotion was scarier than outright rage, and my nerves fluttered as she schooled her mouth into a line. "This is bad, Robin."

You don't say. "The sceptre's no use to her—you know that. She's a Reaper, and all her monstrous allies are scared to death of it."

Even the demons, in fact.

"That's why we can steal it back," added Tansy. "She won't keep it with her. I bet she left it in the coven headquarters."

"Might have."

And we already knew she wasn't there. Temptation seized me. If not for that pesky shield she'd put over the town, I could have used a transportation spell to hop in and out— reclaim it without anyone knowing. But what if she'd left some other nasty surprises behind for me? There was no way she'd taken *all* her monsters into the police station with her. Dammit, I couldn't take the risk.

"If anyone's going back there, it's me," said Ramsey. "Seth's still barricaded in my office, and the others... he hasn't heard a word from them."

There came a knock on the door. Ramsey and Mum both went for their wands, while Tansy leapt in front, putting on an exaggerated kung fu pose. I reached for my own wand as I approached the door and peered through the spy hole.

"Hey, Perry." I yanked the door open, saying over my shoulder, "No need to panic. It's just the Wardens."

She hadn't brought the others with her, but at least it didn't look like she'd picked up a Reaper-shaped shadow either.

"Sorry I took so long." Perry entered the flat and took the armchair I offered her, not in the least concerned by the apparent squalidity. "Linnea left a trail of chaos behind her at the jail, but I think they have it more or less under control."

I grimaced. "Good, because she's now infiltrating *our* jail. It's the first place she went. Possibly to find allies."

"Oh." Her gaze slid to Ramsey, whose hand clenched around his wand. "You're going back?"

"We're getting my dad and his family out first," I said. "They live right on the brink of the forest."

"Oh, man." She scanned the room and did a double take. "Wait, you have two squirrels now?"

"This is Radcliffe," I explained. "He claims he wants to help us stop Linnea."

"But he's untrustworthy," said Ramsey. "He's worked with our enemies in the past."

"Not the Reapers," I hastened to add. "He also looks almost the same as Tansy, and he's volunteered to distract her attention if need be."

"And she's welcome to use him as target practise," Tansy said.

"I'm sitting right here," Radcliffe objected. "I told you I wanted to make it up to you, didn't I?"

Perry blinked in confusion. To her, of course, their entire conversation sounded like nothing more than a series of increasingly aggravated squeaks.

"Never mind them." I pulled out my phone and checked the latest message from Harvey. "Dad's family members are shifters. They can run through the woods while Harvey helps

Dad escape on his broomstick. That's the only way around Linnea's shield spell."

"They'll still be exposed," Perry said. "We'll have to move fast."

"We?" I echoed. "The Wardens will help?"

"Sure," she said. "Helping one family escape is more doable than bringing down Linnea's entire army. I'll ask Tam."

I smiled gratefully. "I'd really appreciate that."

I wanted to rescue them myself, but while Perry was hardly Linnea's favourite person, she wasn't the one against whom the ex-Reaper bore an eternal grudge. Moreover, Linnea's attention was clearly elsewhere.

She got out her phone. "Tam's been helping at the jail. The local branch is on top of things, so we don't have to get involved, but Tam has this thing about tying up loose ends."

"I don't blame him, to be honest." Look at the chaos my family had caused in their habit of leaving all their problems for the next generation to deal with. "You're sure the rest of the team's up for it, though? They were pretty worn out after the fight with Linnea."

"Farley's tougher than she looks, and Callum bounces back easily," she said. "And Maurice is… well, Maurice. He'll complain, but he'll help."

"Good." I typed a message to Harvey. "I think the best move is for you to wait outside the forest to transport my dad and the others here. That way you won't have to engage in any direct fighting with Linnea's monsters."

"Unless some are still roaming in the woods," she added. "Tam will do a sweep of the area before we go in, or one of your squirrels can scout ahead."

"I will," said Tansy and Radcliffe in unison.

My phone buzzed. Harvey had already reached Dad's cottage, and they were ready to leave when I gave the word.

"Tam says he's already there, the overachiever," Perry remarked, her phone in her hand. "He and the others must have transported themselves straight back to the forest."

I blew out a breath then addressed Radcliffe. "If you can really be trusted, you'll go with the Wardens to help them find their way through the forest and warn them if there are any monsters lurking around."

He'd have an incentive—namely, that turning on the Wardens would be far more likely to end disastrously for him than for Perry and the others, given the Wardens' expertise in fighting magical monsters.

"Of course." Radcliffe bounced enthusiastically on his feet. "I won't let you down."

"You'd better not," Tansy growled. "If you come back with Linnea on your tail, I'll feed you to the monsters myself."

"I'll make sure he doesn't cause trouble," Perry told me. "Let's roll."

She left the flat, Radcliffe bounding behind her. In response to Tansy's reproachful look, I muttered, "I value your safety more than his. Also, I didn't want to hear you two arguing the whole time the Wardens are gone."

Not that it wouldn't have been a distraction from worrying about whether the Wardens had run into trouble. Harvey wouldn't be able to text me while on a broomstick, and the Wildwood itself tended to scramble phone signals even when there wasn't a Reaper and her monsters roaming around in there.

Ramsey made to follow Perry, and so did I. Then we looked at one another, shrugged, and walked back to our corresponding armchairs. A minute later, I had to leap up and stop Tansy from climbing out of the window in a bid to follow Radcliffe. Mum didn't try to leave, but the expression on her face could have turned the depths of hell into an ice rink.

I occupied myself by sending Rowan messages, to which she replied with increasingly exasperated emojis just to reassure me that she was all right. Piper, meanwhile, offered to go back to the house under the pretext of trimming the rosebushes and find some way of concocting a poison to use on Linnea.

I put the idea to the others, and we were arguing about the logistics when my phone buzzed with a message from Harvey saying he was on his way here—with Dad.

Part of me remained tense until there came a knock on the door, and I found Perry on the other side again. This time, Harvey stood beside her, his dark hair windswept and tousled and his clothes wrinkled from the flight.

I threw myself into his arms, not caring that my brother and mother were in full view. "I'm glad you're okay. Where's…?"

"I dropped your dad off with Jessica and the kids," he explained. "I don't think he's a fan of flying."

"Oh, right." I should have guessed. "And Jess and the kids?"

"The Wardens are taking them to a hotel in a nearby town," said Perry. "Tam is getting them settled."

My shoulders slumped with relief. "Thanks. I owe you one."

Perry waved goodbye, while Harvey followed me into the flat. "Is this where you're hiding out?"

"Not for long," I said. "Linnea doesn't know this place exists yet, but it's not hard to look up my past addresses, especially if she has my aunt on her side."

"She doesn't, does she?" He looked alarmed. "I know she went to the jail, but didn't she try to kill your aunt and cousin not long ago?"

"I don't know for sure," I added with a glance at my brother. "Did you see Rowan? Or Piper?"

"I didn't," Harvey said. "Piper isn't likely to be a target, is she? I mean, she's employed by your family, but so are a lot of other people."

"Yeah, and Linnea locked the entire council in the coven's headquarters," I said.

As for Rowan, her messages told me in no uncertain terms that she had no intention of leaving town.

A streak of red darted through the window, prompting Tansy to jump up with a loud squeak. "You!"

"I'm here to report!" Radcliffe announced. "After I helped the Wardens find their way through the forest, I had a look around Wildwood Heath. She hasn't gone near your house yet."

"Would she have a reason to? It's not like I left anything valuable in there."

I *had*, technically. But Linnea would have no reason to steal my new camera or Mum's TV. Her interests were in far more valuable prizes.

"And the coven headquarters?" I asked. "Did you look around there?"

"I peeked through the window," he said. "Everyone sitting at the council's table is frozen. Totally frozen. It's really dark too. I could hardly see anything."

A chill raced down my own back. "I bet it's a Reaper trick. Poor Chloe."

Mum spoke up, her voice intent. "And the sceptre—did you see it?"

"No." Radcliffe's tail drooped. "I did look around, but I didn't see any signs of it."

"The sceptre?" Harvey echoed. "Linnea stole it?"

"I dropped it." My heart sank all over again at the disappointment on his face, even though he was among the least likely people to judge me for my mistakes. "Linnea grabbed my hand when I used a transportation spell to get us away from the forest. I guess it's too much to hope that she left it behind."

"I didn't see it anywhere near the forest," he said. "I'm sorry, Robin."

"Linnea probably put it somewhere out of the way." *I hope.* I'd decisively claimed the sceptre for a second time only recently, but my certainty in its choice of me as its wielder was fraying with every moment without it in my hands. What kind of Head Witch *lost* the symbol of their title and power?

"I agree," said Harvey. "I don't see her keeping it on her—not if she can't use it."

"And it scares the demons," I added. "If you ask me, we should call the other Head Witches. This seems like something they ought to know about."

"No," Mum said sharply. "Asking for their help will only make us vulnerable to further manipulation. Moreover, there is little more humiliating to a Head Witch than admitting they've lost their sceptre."

My insides pitched downward, but I glared right back. "I feel like the apocalypse should be a time when one puts saving face on hold. Anyway, not all the Head Witches will see this as a chance for a power grab, and the ones who do will get a rude wakeup call if Linnea decides to turn on them next."

And she might. People like her were never satisfied with a mere taste of power. They always wanted more.

On the other hand, I couldn't say I trusted all the other Head Witches much more than I did Linnea. I didn't think any of them were hungry enough for power that they'd resort to murder and extortion, but that didn't mean they wouldn't be waiting to take advantage of my coven's perceived weakness to stake their own claims. They had sceptres of their own, as well as other notable advantages—such as the Seeing Stone.

"It's too risky," Mum said. "No Head Witch can be trusted."

"Jemima can." She was the one Mum had taken me to when she needed a Head Witch to help me adjust to the position without undermining or exploiting the newbie. "The others, though… they have the Seeing Stone."

The Stone was a relic shared among Head Witches. It functioned like a crystal ball that anyone could use to catch a glimpse of the future. That type of magic was usually open to Seers alone, and while the images the Stone showed were murky to say the least, I was in dire need of some reassurance that I even *had* a future. I preferred one in which I handed Linnea back to the Wardens, found the sceptre, and banished those demons for good.

"Jemima isn't the one with the Stone," said Mum. "We can't take the risk, not if the Stone is in the hands of someone who might exploit our situation."

"How long do we have before it goes public anyway?" I asked. "If we have the narrative in our own hands, we can at least control what gets out there. I've done it before."

Not that Mum had been impressed when she'd woken from her coma to find I'd called the reporters and given them an account of my aunt's crimes to expose them to the world. While that had worked out in our favour, this was an entirely different situation that required someone with a wand—or rather… a sceptre—not a microphone.

When the other Head Witches and I had put our efforts together beforehand, we'd been more than a match even for Linnea's legion of monsters. Mum might not agree with me, but the only way to get that sceptre away from Linnea might be to enlist the help of someone with a sceptre of their own.

4

Mum refused to budge. After I'd bounced off that metaphorical wall a dozen times, we fell into an awkward silence, and it swiftly became apparent that four humans and two squirrels were far too many to squeeze into my tiny flat.

"I need some air," I announced, standing. "Coming, Harvey?"

"Sure." Harvey looked relieved, too, but as I'd predicted, the other two voiced objections.

"You can't go outside," Mum said. "You'll be exposed."

"I'm going to check on Dad. I can take one of the Wardens with me." I indicated the window, from which we could see Perry and the others busy setting up security spells outside our building.

Mum watched through narrowed eyes. "Are you sure those people can be trusted?"

"They helped us, didn't they?" I pointed out. "They also helped me expose Aunt Shannon while you were in a coma."

At my words, her eyes narrowed even further. "We don't know these people, Robin."

"They're Wardens. Defeating magical criminals and their monsters is kind of their thing." I beckoned Harvey after me and walked to the door. "You and Ramsey can talk over our options," I told him.

Whatever *they* were. Mum's penchant for protecting our family's reputation had almost cost her her life more than once, and while she might have had a point about certain Head Witches taking advantage of the situation, I refused to regret bringing the Wardens into this. When we stepped outside, Harvey and I found Perry and Farley in the process of casting a complex shielding spell over the building.

"Don't worry, you can still use transportation spells," Perry said, waving her wand with a flourish. "Didn't realise that would backfire quite that badly."

"I didn't know Linnea even knew the regular kind of magic," I remarked. "I mean, I knew she was half witch, but I've never seen her use a wand."

That was another reason I hadn't realised her link to the Wildwoods' history—aside from my family being the worst communicators on the planet.

"You want to check on your dad?" she guessed. "I can take you to the hotel where they're staying. Maurice and Callum are on guard duty there."

"Thanks." I beckoned to my familiar. "Tansy, can you make sure neither Mum nor Ramsey tries to sneak out while I'm not here?"

Tansy pouted. "Do I have to?"

"Do you trust Radcliffe to?" As predicted, that worked, and she scurried up the drainpipe to the window to perch on the ledge.

"You think they might leave?" asked Perry.

"We have this irritating habit in my family of trying to deal with everything alone and not asking for help when we need it."

"Speak for yourself," Harvey said half-jokingly, sliding his hand into mine as we walked away. "I was starting to worry that I'd get here and find you'd gone."

"Hey, I don't have a death wish." Though being without the sceptre made me feel more vulnerable than I'd expected now I was out in the open. "I'm hoping Ramsey and Mum have a change of heart about bringing the other Head Witches on board while I'm not around."

"There are more of you?" asked Perry, sounding intrigued. "More Head Witches?"

"Not in the immediate area," I replied. "Mum will probably come around to the idea of calling Jemima, I think, but the others… not so much. We might need their help, though."

"And they all have sceptres?" Perry guessed. "Yeah, I can see that being an advantage, but not if they use them against you. I assume that's what your mother thinks will happen?"

"No, it's more of a reputation thing." I pulled a face. "Most Head Witches would sooner get eaten alive by ghasts than admit they made a mistake. As the sole exception, I'm an eternal embarrassment, and that was *before* I managed to drop the sceptre."

"I bet they'd be singing a different tune if it was one of them that Linnea went after," Perry said. "She doesn't want that sceptre of yours, though?"

"She can't use it," I replied. "Nobody but the Head Witch can, and it's been in my family for generations."

The irony was that I'd been doing my level best to get rid of the sceptre since it had claimed me. Like all sceptres, it had been created by the first covens a thousand or more years ago, and its history was bound up with my family so thoroughly that any witch who broke that tradition would be a pariah forevermore. I'd been on the brink of doing exactly that—and I'd already broken the mould in a thousand ways since I'd taken the title of Head Witch—but now there was nothing I wanted more than to have the sceptre back in my hands.

Perry offered to take us to the hotel via transportation spell. I hesitated a little before accepting, recalling her admission to not being the most skilled at that type of spell, but I figured it was the best way to avoid picking up a tail.

A wave of her wand carried us away, straight into a nearby field some hour's distance from the hotel. Perry was all apologies, but frankly, I didn't mind walking. While my brain had entirely too much time to ruminate on my many mistakes during the winding route through the hills, the exertion also dimmed some of my burning desire to run back to Wildwood Heath and make Linnea sorry. At the very least, I needed a proper plan, preferably one that wouldn't fall apart the instant I put it into action.

The issue, of course, was that planning was not remotely my forte. I usually needed Chloe for that—and thinking of my assistant kicked off another wave of guilt. Luckily, Linnea had only put her and the others under a spell and hadn't killed them outright, but who knew what kind of mess she'd created at the police station?

Seeing Dad always cheered me up, even in our current dire circumstances. He came to meet us downstairs in the hotel's seating area since the boys were enacting some kind of wild game of hide-and-seek upstairs with their mother.

"We told them we were taking a surprise holiday," Dad said in explanation. "They got on board a little too enthusiastically, I admit, but it's better than panicking."

"Definitely." A remote town like this wouldn't even be on Linnea's radar. "Mum and Ramsey are at my old flat. Not ideal, but it's the best I've got, and Tansy's there to make sure they don't get ideas about running back to Wildwood Heath."

"Good idea," he said. "They don't mind staying there for a few days?"

"I really hope it's no longer than that." I let my head droop, my energy flagging. "There's being sensible, and there's being a coward, and I don't know where the line is. If I hadn't lost the sceptre…"

"Hey." Dad put an arm around me. "Don't blame yourself —and don't let anyone else blame you either. This isn't on you. It never should have been."

My eyes stung. Dad always had my back, even now, after I'd thoroughly upended his life.

"Linnea is marching around Wildwood Heath as if she owns the place because I couldn't stop her. The only reason I was able to get you out is because, for some reason, she went to the police station first rather than going after my other family members."

"The police station?" His forehead scrunched up. "What was she doing—looking for allies?"

"I bet she was, and it wouldn't surprise me if my aunt talked her way out of her cell." I grimaced. "I'm sure Aunt Shannon would be ecstatic if she found out I left the sceptre behind."

"The sceptre rejected her," Harvey said. "Don't forget that. And Linnea can't use it."

"I can't imagine she wants to carry it around everywhere," Dad said. "If she's left it somewhere, do you think you might be able to send someone in to steal it back while she's not looking?"

"I thought of that, but nobody can step in and out of a room without being seen except a Reaper."

I *did* know a Reaper, but after Mum's reaction to the mere suggestion that I contact another Head Witch, she'd probably start breathing fire if I suggested calling Linnea's considerably less murderous counterpart.

Harvey caught my eye. "You want to call Maura?"

"I do, but Linnea is the last Reaper we trusted, and look at how that turned out."

"Ah." He winced. "Maybe not, then. Still, there might be something to the idea of sneaking into the town behind her back. We know flying isn't affected by that binding spell she used."

"Don't you even think about it," I said. "I'll have my hands full keeping Mum and Ramsey from sneaking out overnight as it is."

Speaking of whom, we'd need to walk back soon if we wanted to reach the flat before dark, so Dad and I said our goodbyes, and Harvey and I headed out of the hotel. Now that I'd been here in person, I'd be able to get back via a transportation spell, though I'd have to be careful not to let Linnea follow me if she did find my hiding place.

Harvey studied my face as the hotel's door closed behind us. "Are you okay?"

"Of course not." I checked my phone again. "A message from Rowan. She's at work—my cousin is. Linnea hasn't shown up yet."

Might Aunt Shannon have kept her mouth shut for once? Or was Linnea not interested in my extended family after all? That she hadn't even tried to lure me back to Wildwood Heath *or* track me down was suspicious, to say the least, and only made me more concerned about what exactly she was doing at the jail.

"We can send someone to get her out," Harvey said. "*I* can get her out, in fact."

I shook my head. "She's refusing. Says that she can spy on the enemy from the inside. Since she's related to the wrong side of the family, it's possible that Linnea will think she's no more my friend than Vanessa is, but that's enough of a danger on its own."

I understood why Rowan was reluctant to leave her job

when she also lived above the cafe where she worked—Harvey was running the risk of getting himself into trouble with his boss the longer he stayed out of town too—but I couldn't let her endanger herself on my account.

"Yeah." His expression clouded. "Maybe call her when her shift is over. She's probably limited in what she can say or do with customers around."

"I can't believe people are buying lattes while the town's occupied by a revenge-crazed Reaper." *Now that I mention it, I want one too.*

The notion of not being able to visit my favourite café again was yet another incentive to drive Linnea out of Wildwood Heath as soon as possible.

Perry came to meet us outside the hotel, pocketing her phone. "I just checked in with Tam. He gave us the go-ahead to play security guard at your flat and the hotel overnight."

"Thanks. I owe you one."

"Hey, it's our prisoner who's rampaging around your home," she pointed out. "Sorry, bad choice of words. I mean, it's our prisoner who's currently having civilised discussions with your coven… that doesn't really work either, does it?"

"Nope." That almost got a smile out of me, if just because the image of Linnea sitting down at a coven meeting was so alien. "I'll see if Mum's come to her senses."

We both cast transportation spells to carry us back to the flat. This time, I took charge of transporting Harvey and me, recalling our slight misadventure earlier when Perry had cast the spell. A good decision, as it turned out. While the pair of us landed right outside the building, Perry somehow transported herself on top of the rack where a bunch of people had parked their broomsticks. She yelped and swore, trying to disentangle herself from sharp twigs while Tansy came scurrying down the drainpipe to join us.

"I'm so glad you're back," Tansy said. "It's so *awkward* in there. Nobody is talking, and that awful squirrel is strutting around because nobody will throw him out."

"Everything all right?" I asked Perry, who pulled another twig from her hair. "You know, maybe you should invest in a broomstick instead."

"Nah, I prefer the direct route… no offence," she added to Harvey, who grinned. "Anyway, Farley and I will be back later, but I think Tam wants us to check in at the office to make sure our reports are accurate."

"Reports?" Suspicion flared. "Tam didn't have to tell them everything, did he? Even me losing the sceptre *and* my town to Linnea?"

"I convinced Tam to gloss over the details, but if he requests a backup team, that's bound to trigger a request for more information."

Ack. "I probably shouldn't tell my mother that. That's not going to make her any more inclined to accept your help."

Then again, if she refused to entertain the idea of asking the other Head Witches, it was either the Wardens or Maura.

I braced myself and walked back into the building. After climbing the stairs, I entered the flat to find Mum and Ramsey sitting in a very awkward silence, neither looking at the other, while Radcliffe perched demurely on the windowsill.

"How many times did one of you try to sneak out while I was gone?" I couldn't help asking.

"Seven," Tansy supplied. "Maybe eight. I went out to chase a pigeon, and Radcliffe took over."

"You trust him now?" I raised a brow.

"I most certainly do not."

"Uh-huh." I sank onto the sofa so that Harvey could claim the other armchair instead of sitting next to my mother. "Did you come to an agreement?" I asked Mum.

"I will call Jemima," she said. "But nobody else."

"No other Head Witches," I surmised. "You don't think Jemima can take on Linnea alone, do you? Because the alternatives would involve asking for a backup team from the Wardens, which requires them to file a detailed report of everything currently going on in Wildwood Heath for permanent record—"

"No."

"Or calling Maura," I said, undeterred. "Since, as a Reaper, she's probably the person who stands the best chance of beating Linnea."

"Absolutely not." Ramsey all but snapped in reply. "To think you'd suggest that after what Linnea did."

"Maura has absolutely nothing to do with her," I said. "She's also not an official Reaper, so there'll be no need to worry about paperwork. *And* she can sneak into town and steal the sceptre back without even being seen. Nobody else can do that."

A muscle ticked in Mum's jaw. I could see her working over the various options in her head, as well as calculating exactly how much of a reputational hit I'd take in pursuing them, before she ground out, "Fine. Contact your friend. Do *not* say you lost the sceptre, and don't say she drove you out of town either."

"Maura really doesn't care—you know that." I went outside to call her, but I got only a dial tone in response. *Must be busy.* I fired off a message and returned to the flat to find Mum had gone into the bedroom to call Jemima. I tuned her out, far from in the mood to listen to her talking about me behind my back.

"Got any new messages?" I asked Ramsey. "From Seth?"

"No." His fingers dug into the sides of the armchair. "Last I heard, he was locked in my office, listening to her setting all the prisoners free."

"What did she do with the other officers?"

"At a guess, she put them under a spell like she did with the council." He spoke through teeth clenched so tightly I worried they'd pop straight out of his mouth. "Everyone is in danger with murderers like Tiffany and Persephone Henbane on the loose."

I swallowed. "Yeah. I know. Linnea must be confident she can keep them in line." Not that her idea of restraint was much to be commended.

His gaze dropped to his phone. "In his last message, Seth asked where you were. I didn't tell him, but I suspect he isn't the only person wondering where the Head Witch has disappeared to."

My face burned. "Tell him I'm getting allies and we're coming to help."

Mum returned from making her phone call and sat back on the sofa. "Jemima will meet us in the morning."

"Morning." The word made my heart sink in my chest. Spending the night away from home felt like conceding defeat, but the sky had already started to darken outside, and it wouldn't do anyone any favours if I ran back to Wildwood Heath while exhausted and got myself killed. "And the other Head Witches?"

"I'm not calling them, Robin. What did the Reaper say?"

"Maura didn't pick up. Something must've come up, so I left her a message." Once she realised how serious the situation was, she'd come straight here, I was sure. "I think she's our best shot to get the sceptre out of Linnea's hands, but the more help we can get, the better."

If Mum didn't soon change her mind on contacting the other Head Witches, maybe Jemima would help me persuade her otherwise.

5

Staying overnight at my flat presented an obvious problem. The flat had one tiny bed, which I offered to Mum, but that left Harvey, Ramsey, and me to negotiate over the sofa and armchairs crammed into the remaining space. Considering my brother was about as relaxed as someone whose rear end had recently met with Prickles the hedgehog, I knew I wouldn't get a wink of sleep in the same room as him, so Harvey and I went to stay at the same hotel as Dad and the others just to have a little privacy for ourselves.

Really, I was impressed by how Dad and Jessica had managed to turn the whole escapade into a fun trip without letting slip to the kids they were fleeing for their lives. They'd handled this far better than I had. So had Harvey. He checked us into a room on the downstairs floor in case we had to flee in the night, though we did have a werewolf and a vampire keeping watch outside on Tam's orders.

So many people were willing to risk their lives to keep my family safe. And I…

Well. The first thing I did when Harvey and I were alone

in the room together was to sink to the floor and burst into tears.

It wasn't my finest hour, I'll say that much. But Harvey listened to my sobbing, offered reassurances, and when that didn't work, he just held me until I'd calmed down enough to scrape together the tattered shreds of my dignity.

"Thanks." I wiped my face with the back of my hand. "God, I'm a mess."

"You're just too used to putting on a brave face." He stroked my hair. "It's not healthy."

"I know that." I gave a weak laugh. "I'm usually the one who tells my family members that. Repeatedly. Now they're rubbing off on me so much that I'm turning into one of them."

"It's not your fault," he said. "Your mother was in a coma. You were saddled with a huge responsibility. Anyone would react the same."

I felt a little better, and I even managed to get some sleep that night. At least until Mum sent me a message at dawn, warning me that Jemima was due to arrive in an hour.

After saying a quick goodbye to a very sleepy Dad and Jessica and two hyperactive kids, Harvey and I returned to the flat and found Tansy on the windowsill, in a standoff with a local grey squirrel. She growled, and the squirrel bolted.

"He could have been a spy," she said in explanation. "I was taking precautions."

"Uh-huh." I rolled my eyes. "Where's Radcliffe?"

"Inside." Her tail twitched in disapproval. "He volunteered to go and entertain your dad's family, but I'm the only red squirrel those kids are allowed to befriend."

"Well, of course."

I put on a smile and walked upstairs to the flat, mentally steeling myself to face my family.

Mum looked more alert than she had the previous day, though Ramsey didn't seem to have slept a wink. He had his phone in his hand and was pacing around the room in an agitated manner.

"Morning," I said to the others, affecting a cheery tone. "When are we meeting Jemima?"

"In an hour." Mum's gaze travelled around the flat. "We need to have this place presentable by then."

"Jemima won't care that a place I'm not even living in isn't a five-star hotel." My own strategy was to make breakfast instead, and since I didn't have any food in the cupboards, Harvey and I had to make a brief excursion to the only nearby corner shop that was actually open at this hour. Trying to make coffee with my ancient second-hand kettle did not improve the mood either, though it gave us something to do other than break into another argument about the merits of contacting the other Head Witches. I didn't blame Tansy and Radcliffe for climbing out the window somewhere between the third and fourth arguments over who got to claim the only coffee mug that wasn't cracked.

"She's here!" Tansy's shout from outside warned me of Jemima's arrival. I looked out the window to see a torrent of silvery stars pursuing a descending broomstick. I wished Mum had warned her to tone it down. Maybe the reason she'd invited Jemima over at this ridiculous hour in the morning was so that there was less chance of her glittering jewellery and shiny hair blowing our cover.

Mum conjured up an extra armchair for her and manoeuvred it into the remaining floor space, and Jemima sat down, clucking her teeth. "Well, Robin, you're in trouble, aren't you?"

"You might say that." I let my guard down—just a bit. Ostentatious dressing habits aside, I could trust her to hold her tongue. "How much did my mother tell you?"

"She told me that Linnea, the rogue Reaper, has broken out of the Wardens' jail and is now occupying Wildwood Heath," said Jemima. "She also mentioned you no longer have the sceptre."

So much for holding the details close to our chest. I looked at Mum, who pointedly avoided my gaze, and then I shrugged. "Yeah, we think Linnea has it. I was casting a transportation spell to get us out, and she closed her hand around it at the last second."

I filled her in on the other details Radcliffe and Harvey had brought us after our rescue attempt, including Linnea's apparent recruitment of Wildwood Heath's entire population of prison inmates.

"She wouldn't be carrying the sceptre around since most afterworld monsters are terrified of it," I finished. "My idea was to sneak in, steal it back, and then use it on her when she's not expecting it."

That would be a lot easier with the help of a Reaper, but Maura had yet to reply to my message. More worryingly, I hadn't heard from Rowan or Piper since the previous night either. I'd sent a message to each of them, but neither was an early riser, so they might not be awake yet.

"You don't think it could have been claimed by someone else?" Jemima asked.

Old insecurities jabbed at me. I pushed them down. "No. My aunt tried to steal it from me recently, and the sceptre definitively chose me again, removing all doubts. The tricky part is figuring out where Linnea put it and getting it back, preferably without her seeing us. That way, we'll have the element of surprise."

"Then you intend to confront her directly?"

"That's the plan." I hitched on a smile. "In theory. She already got the better of all of us, plus an entire team of trained Wardens, so ideally, we need more than one Head Witch—or the equivalent—if we're to pull this off."

Jemima pursed her lips. "Yes, I see. Your mother mentioned you wanted to consult the Seeing Stone. That's an option, since Mavis still has it in her possession, and I believe Mavis herself is also in the region."

"We can talk to Mavis, can't we?" I asked Mum. "We don't have to tell her the full story."

"I doubt you can get away without letting anything slip, Robin."

Kind of harsh. "I can just say that Linnea broke out of jail and is threatening my family. Come on, you know it's important."

"Yes." A moment passed. "As a matter of fact, I already called her this morning."

"You did?" That figured. "What was the point in arguing with me, then? Wait, did you call Acacia and Isadora too?"

"I certainly did not," she replied. "They'd go straight to the press, and both made it quite clear that they will not involve themselves in Wildwood Heath's business again."

Maybe that was for the best. I might not care about maintaining decorum with my life on the line, but involving a pair of gossips whose first move would be to call the local tabloids would be the exact opposite of an effective strategy, however powerful their sceptres might be.

I also didn't need to be burdened with guilt if a certain pair of nosy reporters decided to investigate for themselves and fell afoul of Linnea's monsters too.

"I'll give Mavis another call and let her know we're ready to speak to her," said Mum. "I can't say she'll necessarily want to fight Linnea head-on, but she'll certainly let you gain some insight from the Seeing Stone."

"Good." Admittedly, the Seeing Stone's visions tended to be opaque at best, but it had been a vision I'd seen in the

Stone that hinted at the true reason I'd been chosen as Head Witch in the first place—to banish Grandma's demons and permanently deal with the threat my family had faced for generations.

Within ten minutes, there came another knock on the door. Mum answered, inviting in a grey-haired woman dressed far less outrageously than her fellow Head Witch, with a bright green toad sitting on her shoulder.

"Hello, Robin," Mavis said. "It's been a while."

"Hi, Mavis," I said cautiously. "Thanks for coming here on such short notice."

"Oh, think nothing of it." With a nod of thanks, she took the second armchair Mum conjured and delved into the lacy bag hanging from her shoulder. She pulled out the Seeing Stone. "I believe you wanted to consult this?"

"Thank you." I took the faintly glowing green stone, surprised that she hadn't asked for the details. At a guess, Mum had employed her most fearsome closed-lipped coven leader manner on her when they'd spoken on the phone.

Since I didn't have a table, I placed the stone on my lap and held my hands over its surface.

My vision tunnelled until the flat disappeared in a haze of green light. The forest took its place, and a leafy path vanished beneath my feet as I ran, flanked by shadows on either side. The sceptre in my hand glowed bright, showing the way through the gloom, but the scene was blurrier than the previous time I'd seen it—darker, with shadows shifting and swirling like smoke.

The scene faded. I lifted my head and found the others looking at me expectantly. "It just showed me the exact same as I saw the last time."

"No changes?" asked Jemima. "Nothing at all?"

"It was even less clear than before, if that means anything. Everything was all blurry."

"Really?" Mavis reached out to take the stone back from me. "If that's the case, it's possible the future is changing too rapidly for its visions to reshape around the new turn of events."

"Changing?" My throat went dry. "In what way?"

She wouldn't know, of course, but neither did I. Had Linnea getting her hands on the sceptre changed the future, or something else? Or was I putting too much faith in a vision that I'd never had reason to take seriously in the first place?

Someone knocked on the door.

I jumped to my feet, but Mum beat me to it. After opening the door, she fixed the person on the other side with a glare worthy of a gold medal. "What are *you* doing here?"

"We're here to talk to your daughter, of course." A thin woman entered alongside a taller witch dressed in shining golden outerwear, complete with a hat that resembled a crown.

Isadora and Acacia. They must have followed Mavis. There was no other explanation as to how they'd found their way to my old flat. Mavis herself looked startled, and when I caught her eye, she shook her head, as if to answer my unasked question with *no, of course I didn't tell them to come here.*

"Hello, Robin," said Acacia Bracken, her face creased in its usual sour expression as if she'd swallowed a lemon whole. "I hope you don't mind if I invite myself in."

I did mind. Very much. But if she knew that, she gave no sign. Rather, she planted herself between Mum and Ramsey on the sofa like an honoured house guest.

"I was curious as to why you wanted the Seeing Stone," she said. "Is there a reason nobody at your coven is answering calls?"

Oh. Oh *no.*

"I was curious too." Isadora flounced across the room in a whirlwind of gold fabric and flicked her wand, conjuring up a puffy armchair that made my own furniture look like it had been fished out of a rubbish heap. "When the coven didn't answer, I called the next available number."

Mum stiffened. "My sister."

"Correct," Isadora said. "She claimed you abandoned your post and your sceptre and that she was forced to step in to take over your seat of power. But surely *that* isn't true, is it, Robin?"

My prepared lies unravelled. All the Head Witches stared at me, though Mavis's expression was more sympathetic than Acacia's marked disdain and Isadora's wide-eyed judgement.

With a crack, my self-control snapped. Anger burned through me, and I heard the distinct cries of local birds landing on the roof as my magic reacted to my white-hot rage.

"I did *not* abandon Wildwood Heath," I said heatedly. "Linnea—a rogue ex-Reaper—walked in with an army of afterworld monsters and took the entire coven council hostage. Then she freed every single prisoner in Wildwood Heath, including my aunt Shannon. You saw the recent newspaper articles, surely. You know she's a criminal and a liar."

"I did," said Isadora, "but you don't deny losing the sceptre? And abandoning your post as Head Witch?"

"Linnea stole the sceptre when I was helping my family escape."

Really, Mum could stand to stop glaring at me and stand up for me instead, considering it was her life I'd been saving.

"She also set every dangerous criminal in town free, including the Henbanes, who have also been involved in summoning afterworld monsters in the past. You remember that, don't you?"

They certainly did. Several people had died. Mavis had been attacked by one of those monsters and had been lucky to survive.

"I saw the news," Mavis said. "The evidence was undisputed, Isadora. You saw it for yourself."

"And you must know this isn't the first time Aunt Shannon has taken advantage of a situation like this for her own gain," I said. "She must have been delighted to seize the chance to convince Linnea to cut her jail sentence short. And she must have been even happier when you called and gave her the chance to paint me as the villain."

"You *did* run away, didn't you?" Acacia pressed. "You abandoned the sceptre. That part is true, isn't it?"

"It hasn't even been a day," I said. "We left in order to gather allies before we go back in to drive her off."

"Is that why you called us here?" Isadora said. "You expect *us* to sort out your problems?"

"If I wanted that, I'd have actually invited you here," I said pointedly. "I wanted to consult the Seeing Stone. I have, so you can leave now."

Mum and Ramsey gave me disapproving looks. I ignored them. This was war, and I did not need the judgment of other Head Witches on top of that of my own family members. In any case, Mavis looked somewhat abashed, even if the others didn't.

"You must understand why we're asking questions," said Isadora. "There was a dispute about your fitness to hold the sceptre recently, was there not?"

"No." So much for setting the record straight. "My aunt tried to discredit me, but the sceptre chose me for a second time, and she was arrested and jailed. Didn't you already know that?"

"Nevertheless, no Head Witch would lose a sceptre," said Acacia. "It's unheard of."

My face flamed. I clenched my fists in my lap, determined not to flinch away from her and Isadora's greedy stares.

"It has certainly happened before," Jemima said. "Right, Mavis?"

Mavis nodded. "Yes. Just recently, there was that incident up north where a sceptre was stolen and then retrieved."

Some of the heat faded from my face. "Really?"

Maybe I shouldn't have been surprised. Anyone could theoretically pick up a sceptre, regardless of whether they carried the Head Witch title or otherwise, and it was unlikely that not a single person had ever done so in the centuries they'd been in existence.

"And we certainly aren't begging for assistance," Mum said. "My daughter has proven herself to the sceptre, and we have every intention of returning my sister to jail once we're back in Wildwood Heath."

But I did, against my better judgement, need the Head Witches. Or some of them, anyway. Isadora's flair for the dramatic was often more hindrance than help in a crisis, and she'd treated me with disdain from the start. Acacia, on the other hand, had liked my grandmother. Yes, she didn't have much respect for me, but she was bound to be opposed to the idea of a former Head Witch's ghost being at risk of banishment at the hands of a Reaper.

I took in a breath. "You might have gathered that Linnea has power far beyond a single Reaper. She has an army of ghasts and two demons waiting in the wings, and she trapped our entire council in their headquarters, even Grandma."

"The former Head Witch?" Acacia's eyes grew wide. "That's a terrible indignity."

"She helped us escape," I said, "but I wouldn't be surprised if Linnea banished her to the afterworld to stop her from doing it again."

Acacia looked even more outraged. "You cannot allow that."

"What else am I to do?" Maybe I was pushing a little too hard to win her over, but from her scandalised expression, it might actually work. "I can't bring Grandma here. The only way to stop her from being banished is to drive off Linnea."

Mavis cleared her throat. "I, for one, would gladly offer a helping hand. You said that Linnea had enlisted the aid of various magical monsters?"

"Ghasts, mostly. Like the last time." I suppressed a shudder at the memory of Mavis's own brush with death. "She might have others, though. She freed Tiffany Henbane, and her coven is known to have dabbled with demons."

"That's reason enough to take action," said Jemima. "I gather there isn't time to consult the other Head Witches, given how widespread they are."

That, and we don't want every Head Witch in the country to know I lost the sceptre. Though maybe there were some exceptions. "Yeah, like the ones we met at the gathering up north. Rebecca would probably help, but she's also eleven years old. I'm not dragging her into this."

"Ah, she was also involved in that intriguing case of the stolen sceptre," said Mavis. "Your mother was there, too, in fact. I would have thought she'd have told you."

I swivelled to Mum. "When was this?"

"She paid a visit to the sceptres' original creator over the summer," Mavis said. "She wanted to find out how to unbind your sceptre's magic from you so that you would no longer be Head Witch."

6

M y mouth fell open. "She did *what?*"

My mother had visited the sceptre's creator? And she hadn't *told* me? Questions exploded in my mind like a series of fireworks, and I momentarily forgot that there were four other very curious Head Witches in the room with us. Not to mention my brother. And Harvey, who I wouldn't have blamed for slipping out the room to get away from the inevitable firestorm that was about to result.

Mum must have sensed the same. To the other Head Witches, she said, "I believe that concludes our business here. Have you made up your minds?"

I looked to Acacia first, hoping that Grandma's plight had swayed her, but no luck.

"I'm afraid I am less than convinced by the practicalities of confronting an unknown number of criminals who are allied with a dangerous Reaper," she said.

"Especially now that she holds a sceptre of her own," Isadora said in a rare agreement between the two.

"She doesn't hold the sceptre," I said.

Not that it mattered. My attempt to persuade them had

been doomed from the start, and while I hadn't factored those two in as possible allies, Jemima and Mavis also rose to their feet and began making motions towards the door. Mavis's expression was marked with guilt, but the palpable tension between my mother and me was suffocating enough that I didn't blame her for getting out.

"Call me if you need me," Jemima said before she followed her companion. "I'm afraid that I can't be of much help in an outright fight, but if you need me to contact anyone for you…"

"We should probably keep Rebecca out of this." I might have asked her for more updates on how the young witch was currently dealing with the burden of the Head Witch title, but right now, I was more concerned with getting the details of the latest bombshell Mum had been keeping from me since our trip up north over the summer.

Isadora was the last to leave, clearly not wanting to miss out on the inevitable drama, but her desire to get away from my dingy flat prevailed. When she'd gone, Mum closed the door firmly and shook her head at me. "They might have been persuadable, given enough time."

"You're the one who told them to leave!" I threw up my hands. "You're unbelievable. Is it supposed to be my fault, too, that you met with the sceptre's creator behind my back without telling me?"

"You are being unnecessarily dramatic," she informed me, striding back to the sofa. "I didn't meet the sceptre's *creator*, merely the one surviving witch from the coven who created them."

"Technicalities." A muscle twitched in my jaw. "I would still have liked to know. Was that this summer?"

"Yes, and the friends of the young Head Witch were also visiting her for considerably more urgent reasons," she replied. "They wanted to free her from being bound to the sceptre that chose her as its wielder."

"And you asked for the same for me." My heart sank. "You wanted to know if it was possible to take the sceptre away and give it to someone else. Is that all?"

"You never wanted to wield it," she said. "You wanted to be free, didn't you?"

"You know I did." My eyes stung. "But if that was why you went, you should have given me the choice."

To my surprise, a faint flush appeared on her cheeks. "I confess to it being an impulsive decision on my part, and one that proved irrelevant to our current problems. I learned very little that would have been of any help to you, so I decided you didn't need the distraction."

"That wasn't your call to make." I could feel the fight draining out of me despite my best efforts. We'd spent enough of the day arguing and had walked away with exactly zero new allies and a dozen new grievances instead. "Who exactly did you meet? I mean, the last survivor of an ancient coven must be a powerful witch."

"Adele Primrose," she said. "As she has little of the original gift, she isn't engaged in the activities of the current Head Witches and wields no sceptre of her own."

"She doesn't have one?" Strange. "I didn't know that anyone even knew *who* created the sceptres, let alone that any members of their coven were taking visitors."

"It took some time to track her down," she said. "I went there with someone who needed her help much more than I did. A sceptre was in the hands of someone very dangerous, someone who never should have been able to use it. Adele Primrose confirmed that there is a rare spell that enables someone to unbind a sceptre from its wielder."

For the second time, my jaw hit the floor. "*Anyone* can

unbind a sceptre from its wielder? They don't have to be a Head Witch?"

"Yes, but it's impossible for anyone else to claim a sceptre unless the sceptre itself makes the choice," she said. "In its unbound state, the sceptre would be usable, but there are limitations as to what can be done, depending on the person's experience with a wand."

"Linnea is a witch." *Oh no. Please tell me that's not her plan.*

"She won't have the faintest idea how to go about unbinding a sceptre, even if she knew it was possible, which I very much doubt," Mum said. "I'm told it's incredibly difficult to do even for an experienced witch, and Linnea favours her Reaper side. Like I said, nothing in what Adele Primrose shared with me is relevant to this current situation."

"I still wish you'd told me." My skin crawled at the thought of anyone being able to unbind a sceptre from its wielder against their will. No wonder this Adele Primrose seemingly kept a low profile. "Why'd you decide not to try it with me? Because you assumed that if you managed to unbind the sceptre from me, it would choose me again and not another wielder?"

"Yes, that's the extent of it," she said. "The recent challenge from your aunt confirmed that would have been the outcome. Is that all?"

"Not remotely." My list of questions was stacked as high as the paperwork that had doubtless sprung up in my office during my absence. "Does this Adele Primrose know *how* her ancestors created the sceptres?"

"She said they took the secret to their graves."

That explained why there hadn't been any more created in such a long time.

"And their one survivor isn't a wielder," I said.

This was further proof that the system through which a

sceptre chose its owner was flawed, to say the least—and that even the sceptres' creators had limits.

"Yes," Mum said. "Now we can return to the matter at hand. Linnea."

"Except, you know, you did just kick all our potential allies out of my flat."

"You were making a scene, Robin."

"Don't pin this one on me. If you'd told me the truth in the first place—"

My phone buzzed in my pocket.

I checked the number and saw that Maura was calling. "I'll be right back."

I left the flat, closing the door on Mum's reply, and answered the phone. "Maura?"

"Robin?" she said. "Sorry, I didn't get your message until this morning. I was out with Drew. What happened?"

"Linnea." All my anger and frustration reared up again. "She came marching into Wildwood Heath with an army of ghasts and cast a shielding spell so that nobody can use transportation spells to get in or out. Then she set free every criminal in town."

I heard her swear under her breath. "Seriously? Now I get why your message was so urgent. Are you okay? Where are you hiding?"

"My old flat," I replied. "My family got out and so did Harvey, but everyone else is trapped in Wildwood Heath. Oh, and she also has my sceptre. That's why I needed your help."

"No kidding?" I heard her whisper something along the lines of, "Mart, get your paws off my phone. This is serious."

"Your brother's there?" I guessed. "It might be easier if we talk in person. If you're willing to come, I mean."

"Of course, I am. Linnea is nothing but trouble, both for the Reapers and for everyone else."

Relief flooded me. "Thanks. I really appreciate it."

I rattled off the flat's address and then went outside to check on the squirrels. Neither had returned during our tumultuous meeting with the other the Head Witches, and it took a few minutes of searching before I spied two fluffy tails overhead on the drainpipe.

"What are you two doing up there?" I called.

"We're making a *plan*." Tansy peered down at me. "Have those awful Head Witches finally left?"

"Yes, but Maura's coming next."

Time to drop the bad news on Mum. Or good news, considering we had a distinct dearth of other allies lining up to help us.

Mum must have expended all her energy on our prior argument, because her response was a weary, "It's your choice, Robin."

"Yes, it is." Perhaps that was an attempt at reconciliation over her underhandedness in visiting the Primrose Coven behind my back, and I was happy to call a truce if I was free to ask for help from the one Reaper I trusted not to betray us.

Maura showed up as promptly as I'd expect of a Reaper. While she knocked on the door, Mart drifted straight through the door into the flat and grinned at us. "Nice to see you again."

"Mart, you can't just go barging into people's homes," Maura said from the other side as I opened the door. "Sorry, Robin."

"He's not the most unwelcome house guest I've had today, believe me." I offered her a seat on one of the extra chairs Mum had conjured while Mart zipped around inspecting every corner of the flat.

"This place is a bit of a dump, isn't it?" he remarked. "Reminds me of our old flat."

"Nobody needs your commentary, Mart," said Maura. "So—tell me the worst."

I took in a breath and gave Maura a more detailed account of Linnea's attack and our subsequent attempts to find out what she was up to.

"I don't know if the other Head Witches are coming back," I said. "And the Wardens' hands are tied. They have to report everything to their bosses, so calling in a backup team risks landing us in a whole heap of trouble without any guarantee that they'll actually help."

"They also can't walk through walls," added Maura. "Which is a skill it sounds like you're in need of."

"Are you sure?" I asked. "It's risky. I'm not going to underplay that."

"Oh, she'll do it anyway," said Mart. "She can't seem to help herself."

"A rogue Reaper is likely to make trouble for all of us eventually," Maura pointed out. "I can guarantee I'll already be on her radar since I helped with her arrest. I can go into the town and get the scope of the situation first. How about that?"

"We'll need to figure out where she put the sceptre," I agreed. "Then go in and grab it, if we can."

"Sure," she said. "I think I know your town well enough that I can get in and out using the afterworld, but given that Linnea is also a Reaper, I'd like to avoid crossing her path."

"Better avoid the jail, then." I caught my brother's eye, and his jaw tightened. "As far as I know, that's where she's been hanging around, since she set all the prisoners free, including my aunt Shannon."

"Your aunt was in jail?" Her eyes widened. "Clearly, I've missed a few things. Is she allied with Linnea now?"

"I'd like to hope not, but she's been known to take advantage of any opportunity to undermine me."

Maura had witnessed some of that herself.

"She's certainly not going to go out of her way to fight on my side, at any rate," I said.

"All right." She blew out a breath. "I'll look around the coven headquarters, if you're sure she isn't there. And that she didn't banish your grandmother's ghost."

"I honestly have no idea." I wouldn't have thought she'd let Grandma roam free, but nothing Linnea had done since her arrival in Wildwood Heath had fit with my assumptions. "She's so unpredictable, and it's my family who's at the top of her hit list. Even the dead ones."

"I'll tread carefully," she promised. "Wish me luck."

She and Mart both vanished. I held my breath, already having second thoughts, while Ramsey rose to his feet and began pacing.

"If she doesn't go to the police station, we won't know for sure whether Linnea is there," he said. "Seth hasn't replied to any of my messages since last night. Either she caught him, or he escaped and went on the run."

Or worse. My guilt and worry only heightened when I got a reply in from Rowan claiming that she'd taken my advice to lie low and that she'd also put security spells all over her flat.

I covered the whole café in spiderwebs, she said. *My boss wasn't happy, but I told him an evil Reaper was hunting me. She hasn't stopped by for a latte, anyway.*

That might have got a smile out of me if I hadn't been so wound up. I was about to walk outside to get some air when Maura returned with her brother in tow.

"Your grandmother tried to chase us off," he announced.

"She didn't—did she?"

"I got past her when I made it clear we weren't a threat," Maura said. "You were right. Linnea wasn't in the coven headquarters, but everyone in the council room is stuck in the afterworld. I could have brought them out if I'd had more than a minute, but your aunt came snooping around, so I had to duck out before she spotted me."

"What was she doing?" I scowled.

"Looked like she was checking whether they were still trapped," said Maura. "My brother tried to slip into her office, but it's totally ghost-proofed and covered with booby traps, too, I'm betting. That was the only room we couldn't get into."

"I bet that's where the sceptre is." My hands clenched at my sides. "Did you look anywhere else?"

"Only the building next door," she said. "There were ghasts roaming outside, so I couldn't get close."

"They weren't attacking anyone?" At a guess, they weren't —even Linnea was unlikely to have set her monsters on her own allies. "That's the Henbane Coven's headquarters. You know, the criminals she let out of jail."

"Yeah, I didn't go to the jail," she said. "I can try, but if you think that's where Linnea herself is…"

"Best not risk it." I saw Ramsey trying to catch my eye again and shook my head. "If I can snag the sceptre without her seeing me, we might be able to take her by surprise. Problem is, I also need to get into my aunt's office."

"I can get you in," Maura said. "I can't promise you won't run into any booby traps, but I'll try."

"Speak for yourself." Mart offered a wounded look. "There was so much sage around her office, it feels like it's stuck to me. I'm traumatised."

"I did tell you not to go near that place," Maura said. "Anyway, once she understood I wasn't there to Reap her ghost, your grandmother said she'd be willing to help. I assume she's on your side, not your aunt's?"

"Yeah, she helped us escape." Wonders would never cease. "I'll have to contact the Wardens and see if they're ready."

"Which team of Wardens did you say you're working with?"

"The leader is a guy named Tam."

"No kidding?" Her eyes sparkled. "I'd say you picked exactly the right team for the job, then. Let's go."

7

That Maura had already met Perry and the other Wardens was far from the most surprising revelation of the day, but it kicked off another flurry of questions.

"When was this?" I asked her as we waited for Perry to reply to my message.

"They came to stay at our inn not long ago," she explained. "They'd come to hunt a monster, of course."

"I bet they were interesting guests." In ordinary circumstances, I'd have asked for more details, but we had quite enough monsters to contend with in the present day.

At that moment, Maura spotted our familiar companions sniffing around the windowsill and gave a double-take. "You have two familiars now?"

"He's more of a temporary ally," I said, gesturing to Radcliffe. "And Linnea can't tell the difference between him and Tansy. That's handy."

"I bet." She looked between them. "Yeah, I can't see it either."

"We are completely different!" Tansy squeaked. "I'm taller than he is, and my tail is fluffier."

"Uh-huh." I wouldn't let on that I would have had trouble telling the difference myself if I couldn't understand their speech. "What's your plan, then? You were scheming long enough that you must have figured something out."

"Obviously we're the distraction," Radcliffe squeaked. "While you're grabbing the sceptre, we'll lead Linnea on a wild squirrel chase."

"Sure she'll fall for that?" I asked then conveyed the suggestion to Maura and her brother. "I don't know that she'll abandon her army to go chasing squirrels."

"She might, if she thinks you're with them," Maura said thoughtfully. "We can use that."

At that moment, Perry's reply arrived, saying she was on her way. I could see Mum and Ramsey growing restless, no doubt displeased at the continued stream of visitors, but Maura's arrival had given me a definite confidence boost, and my certainty that Aunt Shannon had brought the sceptre into her office only cemented my determination to get it away from both *her* and Linnea.

A knock soon came on the front door. Perry walked into the flat and offered Maura a smile. "Fancy seeing you again."

"Small world," Maura deadpanned. "You've met our current least-favourite rogue Reaper, then?"

"Unfortunately, yes," Perry replied. "And her army of monsters. You're the one who brought her in before?"

"Robin did a fair bit of the work herself." Maura spotted the rest of the team behind Perry, and her attention lingered on Maurice, her eyes narrowing a little. Reapers weren't fans of vampires, generally. "She didn't cause too much chaos when she broke out of your high-security prison, did she?"

"A fair bit, but she's done a lot worse to Wildwood

Heath's jail," said Perry. "Set every criminal in town free, in fact."

"I know," said Maura. "Robin told me."

The Wardens crowded into the flat—with difficulty—and Maura and I filled them in on what we'd figured out so far.

"I need to get the sceptre back first," I said. "With Maura's help, I can hop in and out of there without Linnea noticing and then strike her from behind."

"Then what?" asked Maurice. "We're the diversion, are we?"

"Not at all." I jerked my head towards Radcliffe. "He's the diversion. He and Tansy have volunteered to keep Linnea busy while I get the sceptre. Then we'll run outside and join the rest of you."

"There are ghasts roaming outside the building," Maura put in. "And the council is under one of those charmingly nasty little afterworld spells. I'll need a little time to set them free, but once I do, our number of allies will go up dramatically."

"Are you sure they'll be in any fit state to fight?" I asked, thinking of Mum slipping into a coma after she'd been held hostage in the afterworld.

The pause that preceded Maura's reply did not inspire confidence. "They might be. I can't promise anything, but I can guarantee she's not currently expecting us. We'll have a head start when we get the sceptre back, and we can take out as many of her allies as possible before she catches on to us."

"Did you forget how hard it is to banish *one* of those beasts, let alone twenty?" Maurice enquired. "One Reaper won't cut it."

"He's right." Mart poked his sister in the chest.

She scowled when his finger went straight through her. "I can handle it."

"I'm not so sure we should be the only Warden team

present," Callum added with a glance at Tam. He'd been quiet throughout our discussion, though it was the intense kind of quiet that signalled he was thinking hard. My brother often did the same.

"It's going to be hard doing this without backup," Tam said. "Also, we can only stay away so long without letting the officials know exactly what Linnea did."

"I know," I said, conscious of Mum and Ramsey glaring daggers at me. "But if we drive her out of town and get the sceptre back, you won't need to mention those parts. I mean, the prisoners she set free in Wildwood Heath are more the responsibility of our own police force, not the Wardens. The sceptre too."

Ramsey inclined his head. To Maura, he added, "Are you absolutely certain you saw the Henbane Coven inside their headquarters?"

"I didn't get a good look up close, but there was definitely someone in there," she said. "Those monsters were patrolling around the building, almost like they were on guard duty."

"They're definitely working together." Worry rose inside me. We'd struggled to take on Linnea and her monsters *before* she'd set the Henbane Coven's criminals free, and it sounded as though the entire coven was now allied with her.

"And the demons?" said Maurice. "Did everyone forget she is working with two demons—that it's child's play for a Reaper to call them to her side from the afterworld?"

All eyes turned to the vampire. The thought *had* crossed my mind, more than once, but it was quite enough to contemplate taking on an army of ghasts without adding demons into the equation.

"They aren't around," Maura supplied. "Not yet. I checked."

"And we're supposed to take your word for it?"

"Knock it off, Maurice," said Callum. "Maura's more than

proven herself trustworthy. What's the plan, Tam? We go in through the forest?"

"Yes, we'll approach from the outside," said Tam. "Together with anyone else who wants to accompany us."

Meaning my mother and brother. And the squirrels. I didn't like the idea of Tansy putting herself in harm's way, but she was insistent, and I had to admit that she and Radcliffe might be capable of causing just the right level of confusion to keep Linnea's eyes away from me while I grabbed the sceptre.

"I'm coming too," said Harvey. "I'll go in with the Wardens."

"And do what?" Harvey was competent enough at magic, but his main skill involved flying, not fighting. I loved him for making the offer, but I wouldn't have asked him to lay down his life for me.

"I'll check on Rowan," he said. "Piper, too, if you know where she is."

"At home, I expect." My heart began to race. "Right. You all go ahead, and then Maura and I will go in through my aunt's office. I'll grab the sceptre and join you. That about cover it?"

"Pretty much," said Maura. "Mart and I can jump back and forth between here and the forest so that we know when to go in. Right, Mart?"

"I don't remember volunteering," Mart said. "Not without compensation."

"I already said you can choose what film we watch on every single movie night for the rest of the year."

"Not enough," he announced. "I want to choose for next year too."

"Right, right." Maura rolled her eyes. "Honestly, you're getting the easy end of the deal on this."

"Unless I get eaten by a horrible monster."

"You're a ghost. That's significantly less likely to happen to you than it is to the rest of us."

Callum looked mildly bewildered by this exchange since he couldn't see or hear Mart.

Neither could Tam, but he took it in stride. "Ready?"

Not in the least.

So many things might go wrong. Aside from Linnea and her own ambitions, there was no telling what the Henbanes might have done since they'd escaped captivity. Given their past pursuits and dodgy dealings, I was sure that they wouldn't easily give up on their newly gained power.

A shrill ringtone sounded. Everyone jumped then looked at Mum, who held up her phone. "It's Jemima."

Was she coming with us after all? I watched Mum duck into the bedroom to answer the call, and Mart floated in pursuit in a not-so-subtle attempt to eavesdrop.

"Stop that," Maura said. "It's not polite."

"Have I ever been polite?" He hovered near the door, a grin on his face. "Sounds like you have another ally or two."

"The other Head Witches?" My heart lifted despite myself. I hadn't completely screwed up after all, though I couldn't say I had faith that *all* of the Head Witches would deign to involve themselves in this mess.

Mum left the bedroom and closed the door behind her. "Jemima and Mavis are willing to come and help us deal with Linnea."

"Isadora and Acacia don't care to lend a hand?"

"Be glad they don't. They'd certainly expose all the unpleasant details of Linnea's attempt to take over Wildwood Heath—including the loss of the sceptre—to as wide an audience as possible."

"And they won't do that anyway?" It wasn't like I cared what the press said as much as Mum and Ramsey did, but I'd prefer for the truth to come out *after* I had the sceptre back, not beforehand.

"Forget that," Ramsey said to my surprise. "Getting back control over Wildwood Heath is our priority. Nothing else."

"Damn right," I said.

When Jemima and Mavis showed up, there was a considerable amount of scrambling to make room inside my already overcrowded living room. Luckily, Mum had conveyed the gist of our plan over the phone, and the Wardens took the arrival of the Head Witches as their cue to leave. They vanished, all using transportation spells except for Maurice, who insisted on sprinting ahead with vampire-induced speed.

When Jemima and Mavis were clear on our strategy, they too departed, together with Mum and Ramsey. I couldn't decide which worried me more—that the exertion would prove too much for Mum or that my brother's penchant for taking on the whole responsibility for the town's criminals would backfire on him if he did anything foolish, like trying to arrest the entire Henbane Coven by himself.

"I'll keep an eye on him," Maura said when I mentioned this. "Who's left?"

"Us," Tansy announced.

Harvey and the two squirrels were the last to leave. I went downstairs to see them off. Harvey would be flying there on his broomstick, and the two squirrels had opted to hitch a ride with him.

Once outside, Tansy jumped onto my shoulder and wrapped her fluffy tail around my neck. "I'll be fine," she said. "She'll never catch me."

Harvey held up his broomstick. "I'll see you on the other side."

I hope that doesn't mean the afterworld.

I hugged him, pressed my lips to his, then let go. The two

squirrels hopped onto his shoulder as he climbed onto the broomstick, and they were off, rising above the rooftops and into the sky.

I returned to the flat to wait, my nerves swarming. Mart had promised to keep an eye out for any trouble the others might run into in the forest, but even a ghost wasn't immune to being harmed by a Reaper. Neither was Maura, come to that, and I was already having second and third thoughts about letting her take me along for the trip through the afterworld.

"Will it hurt?" I asked her when she next returned. "Travelling through the afterworld when I'm not a Reaper?"

"Only if you let go," said her brother helpfully.

Apprehension aside, I already knew what it felt like to stare into the darkness of a place no human was ever meant to set foot in. I'd done it before. I'd *been* there before, when I'd been unwillingly separated from my body. That had been Linnea's doing too.

The far scarier part was that the enemy herself had access to the afterworld, and it was only a matter of time before she noticed another Reaper sneaking around her domain. If we lost the element of surprise, that was it.

According to Maura and Mart's updates, the path through the forest was undisturbed, and Linnea seemed to have kept her monsters within the boundaries of Wildwood Heath itself. Mart had risked a peek at the police station and claimed that some were standing guard outside while others patrolled the road where the coven headquarters lay. I could only hope that the barrier of sage my aunt habitually kept around her office would keep the monsters out too.

When Maura arrived with the announcement that the others had safely reached the town, it was time to go in.

"Don't worry," Mart said cheerfully. "Really, it's not that

scary over here. It's rather relaxing and quiet when there aren't monsters screaming in your ears."

"Not helping." I approached Maura. "Come on, before I change my mind."

"Just try not to panic." Maura reached out a hand.

I took it, and she pulled me into the darkness of the afterworld.

If I lived to be a thousand, I'd never quite come up with the words to do justice to the bizarre sensation of stepping out of this world entirely. Being in the afterworld felt a little like being suffocated—even though I didn't technically *need* to breathe without my physical body, my lungs burned as I gasped for air that wasn't there. I held on tightly to Maura's arm, wishing I had Tansy with me and also glad she didn't have to go through this experience herself. Nothing but dark encircled us. I felt as if all my senses had been completely disconnected from my body.

Maura displayed no fear, no hesitation. She moved with purpose, gliding across that dark desert with me clinging to her side. How she knew where she was going, I had no idea, but after only a few seconds—endless though they might have felt—a window opened in midair. Through that window, I glimpsed a snapshot of the regular world, a full-colour display of a place with normal dimensions and full access to all my senses.

Specifically, the inside of Aunt Shannon's office.

The room didn't look any different than it had during my last visit, with a large desk dominating the centre and shelves lining the edges, stacked high with old books. My aunt sat at the desk, bent over a notepad. Sudden anger jolted through me.

How dare she come straight back here and take over her old job as though she hadn't committed a crime? And what has she done with the sceptre?

I craned my neck, and my gaze snagged on a sheen of purple light at the desk's side. The sceptre lay atop a small bookshelf, doubtless surrounded by invisible booby traps. My hand twitched in that direction all the same.

"Wait," Maura whispered. "We need to get closer."

My aunt couldn't see us on the other side of the window Maura had opened, but the instant I reached from the afterworld into the realm of the living, she'd be treated to the alarming sight of my disembodied hand appearing out of thin air. While her reaction would no doubt be amusing, I didn't want to dive headfirst into a trap.

"Get on with it," Mart griped. "She's ghost-proofed the whole place."

"But she hasn't Reaper-proofed it." Maura froze then uttered a sharp hiss of shock. "Oh no. There's something—"

She vanished, her hand slipping out of mine as she was swallowed by the darkness.

I stared, first at the spot where she'd vanished, then at the office on the other side of the unseen window she'd opened. My sceptre gleamed, tantalisingly close, as belated panic hit me. "Maura?"

No answer, and my hand remained empty as my dilemma slowly sank in. Whatever had caused her to vanish was all but certainly Linnea's doing, which suggested she knew we were here. More to the point, Maura's departure left me on the wrong side of the dark curtain between the worlds of the dead and the living.

I was stuck in the wrong realm with a Reaper who wanted me dead.

8

I took in a breath that I didn't technically need to take and received a lungful of nothingness in return. Choking on panic, I tried to get a grip on the situation. Maura was gone, but with the real world just a step away, maybe I could cross into it and take the sceptre without needing Maura's help. Of course, I'd probably run afoul of whatever magical defences Aunt Shannon had put on her office, but anything was better than being stuck in this freezing hole, waiting for Linnea and her monsters to find me.

Aunt Shannon hadn't even looked up from her desk. She continued to scribble on her notepad, oblivious, as the window to the world below began to fade around the edges. *Oh no.*

I leaned forward, trying to see a way to get to the sceptre that did not involve face-planting onto my aunt's desk. Nope. This was going to hurt.

All right then. I braced myself and jumped.

Something seized my arm. Or rather, some*one*. Linnea's

face appeared out of the shadows, and her hand locked around my wrist, pulling me back into the darkness.

"Your Reaper friend left you here, did she?" She smiled wickedly. "I'm going to enjoy this."

"What did you do to her?" I squirmed, trying to free myself, but the strength of her grip coupled with the disorientating sensation of hovering in midair made it even harder to break her hold. Worse, I could see the window into the world below shrinking with every passing moment.

The sceptre. It was right there in my aunt's office, just out of reach. I strained towards it, teeth gritted.

"Let me *go!*" I yelled, reaching out with my free hand.

My fingers brushed the window and passed straight through. Aunt Shannon leapt to her feet with a shriek, and a dozen flashes went off as her security spells kicked in. One of them hit my outstretched hand and sent an electric shock through my limbs—then I felt Linnea's grip on my arm break as I tumbled headfirst out of the afterworld.

I hit my aunt's desk with a thud that sent a wave of pain through my right elbow and shoulder, then I rolled off. My hand burned from the spell's shock, and sparks danced before my eyes. Another series of flashes dazzled me, and my aunt's shrieking indicated that she'd ended up in their path too. Shielding my eyes, I stumbled to my feet.

I didn't make it two steps before something akin to a giant cobweb locked around my feet and began climbing up my ankles.

"Hey!" I kicked out, succeeding only in entangling myself even further in the sticky webbing.

"How dare you!" Aunt Shannon shouted, batting away a second curtain of webs that had landed directly on her head. "How dare you break into my office?"

"You're supposed to be in a cell." I reached into my pocket and grabbed my wand as the webbing climbed up to my chest. With a flick of my wrist, I cast a reversal spell that loosened the webbing around my legs.

When my feet were free, I lunged towards the sceptre. The instant my fingers brushed against the sceptre, the gem on its end lit up with violet light. At the same time, a series of ropes sprang into existence and tightened around my arm. As I'd suspected, my aunt was not going to let me reclaim the sceptre without a fight.

"This—is—*mine.*" I clung onto the sceptre despite the growing pain in my arm. "Aunt Shannon, turn off your booby trap spells."

"How do I know you're the real Robin?" she said. "You could be an impostor. Or possessed by a demon."

"Demons are scared of this." I gave a final tug on the sceptre, and purple light ignited, sending a wave of violet throughout the room. The crash of shelves falling filled the background as I shook the ropes free then slid my wand up my sleeve so I could properly grip the sceptre with both hands.

With the path clear, I ran for the door, pursued by my aunt's screaming.

"You can't ruin my office and then disappear! Fix this mess at once, Robin."

"Now you believe who I am?" I spun on her, my anger reaching a crescendo. "Then you know exactly what I think of you stealing my property while I was gone."

"I was protecting the sceptre, not stealing it," she objected. "Really, you should be thanking me."

A crash came from outside the building, then a louder one, followed by the ominous growling that I knew belonged to the ghasts. *Oh no.* Maura had vanished, and with Linnea present as well as her monsters, the others would need my help.

"Get back here!" my aunt yelled as I stepped over the

threshold. "Robin Wildwood, if you still want any shreds of your reputation to remain intact when this is over—"

I slammed the door in her face and cast a locking spell for good measure. She might be one of the more accomplished witches in the coven, but I expected her to run away before she'd offer any help against the ghasts. My aunt was on nobody's side but her own.

I ran for the stairs. The noise from outside grew louder, growls distinguishable amid the fizz and spark of spells being cast and the general racket that could only be a magical battle.

I reached the lobby and ran out of the coven headquarters to a scene of absolute chaos. The Wardens battled Linnea's ghasts, joined by a few witches and what looked like half the police force. Ramsey and Mum duelled side by side, the latter shouting commands at a group of witches they must have picked up along the way.

I lifted my sceptre and ran to join the fray, firing off a spell that hit two ghasts—and accidentally caught Maurice. The sight of the vampire in freeze-frame made Perry laugh, but she hastily stifled her reaction when Tam ran in to check on them.

"Sorry." I cast a reversal spell on the vampire, who broke free with a snarl of fury. "I didn't do that on purpose."

"She really didn't," Perry added and cast a freeze-frame charm of her own. A wand lacked the sheer firepower of a sceptre, but it was enough to halt the ghast advancing on her. "We set up a sage circle near the main path in the forest. We need to herd the beasts over there."

"Gotcha." I lifted my sceptre and levitated the frozen ghasts down the street, further disrupting the ongoing fight. "Where's Linnea?"

"No idea. I thought she was with you—and Maura."

Maura.

"They must be in the afterworld." There was nothing I could do to help her, so I continued to levitate the ghasts until we came to a line of sage just within the forest's boundary. Farley and Callum stood guard beside it, as did several police officers.

"Who set you free?" I asked of Seth, who looked no worse for wear for having spent the night locked inside my brother's office.

"That'd be those squirrels of yours." He gestured to a nearby tree in which I could see two fluffy red outlines. "Your brother convinced them to stay out of the battle."

"Good." I ducked as a spell flew over my head, aimed at a ghast that had tried to slip out of the circle of sage. While they'd be able to break out if they were persistent enough, the limited space made it easy for us to drive them back again, and Linnea's absence meant nobody was giving them direct orders.

That can't last.

I ran back to the coven headquarters and cast a freezing charm on another ghast that ran into my path. Veering around its body, I spied a larger beast attempting to break through the doors to the coven headquarters.

"Is Grandma not around?" I ran past my mother, casting a spell that knocked the beast several feet back. Mum looked tired, but the number of witches she'd called in to help ensured that the bulk of the work didn't fall on her.

"She's the one who brought in our backup," Mum said. "She's been recruiting half the coven while we've been gone."

"Lucky Linnea didn't notice." *Where is she?*

If Maura had engaged her in a fight in the afterworld, I couldn't say for sure who'd come out on top. It depended on whether Linnea had managed to summon those demons.

And now that I had the sceptre back in my hand, I had to confront the growing possibility that the risks I'd overlooked in my quest to get it back might come back to bite me.

A ghost flew past and crashed into the wall of the coven headquarters with enough force to shatter glass.

I ducked as shards rained down. "I hope that was Aunt Shannon's window."

"So do I." Rowan stepped into view, her wand in hand. "It'd serve her right."

"What are you doing here?" I asked my cousin.

"Not missing out on the fun." She flicked her wand again and sent the ghost flying head over heels down the street, then the Wardens moved in to herd it into the sage circle with the rest. They certainly moved with efficiency, but *banishing* those beasts would be another matter entirely, even with two Head Witches present. I glimpsed Jemima and Mavis fighting alongside the coven witches, their sceptres aglow.

Darkness swept overhead, swift and sudden. Fear gripped me, and I lifted the sceptre, its purple sheen penetrating the gloom. Amid the dark, I glimpsed two figures grappling, though that isn't quite the right word to describe the sight of two Reapers going head-to-head. They fought like a pair of angry cats—albeit cats made of pure shadow—and coldness radiated from them like someone had turned a freezer up to max and left the door open.

Linnea broke away first, and when she spotted me, she offered a smile. "Not bad at all, Robin. I knew you'd be more than a match for my ghosts."

"What's your game?" I waved the sceptre, casting a spell that she deflected with a mere flick of her wrist. Shadows cloaked her, repelling any magic that tried to touch her. "You've lost, you know. Your monsters are outgunned."

"You know, I never really *wanted* to take over Wildwood

Heath," she said. "Your cowardly act of abandoning your home was an opportunity, but I've always had grander ambitions."

"What is that supposed to mean?" I saw Maura creeping up on her from behind, but in the same instant, Linnea spotted her too.

"Your council will never catch me," Linnea said. She turned to the other Reaper. "Neither will you."

"We'll see about that." Maura reached out to grab her, but Linnea darted aside and vanished into the darkness before reappearing several feet away from us.

"The game's just starting, Robin," she called out. "I'll be back."

She disappeared as dozens of spells flew in her direction, colliding in a bright flash that banished the remaining shreds of darkness.

"I'll be back?" Mart laughed derisively. "That's really the best line she could come up with?"

"You're alive," I said. "Or—you know what I mean."

"Let's not go there," Maura muttered. "Also, I don't trust that she's gone."

Neither did I. She'd left utter chaos behind her, and while most of the ghasts had been rounded up and tossed into the circle of sage, the road was a mess of broken glass and brick and the erratic effects of misfired spells.

"Also, I'm sorry, Robin," Maura added. "I didn't mean to leave you in the afterworld."

"Was it Linnea who grabbed you?"

"Yeah," she said. "Nearly had me too. It's lucky she didn't have those demons with her."

"And the Henbanes."

Why hadn't *they* shown their faces? Most were cowards, admittedly, but I would have expected Tiffany at least to play a role in the fighting or force her apprentices to stand in her place.

Maura peered approvingly at the pile of ghasts heaped inside the sage circle. "Nice work. Shouldn't be too hard to banish them with five sceptres between us."

"Five?" I followed her gaze down the street, which contained considerably fewer ghasts than before and considerably more Head Witches. Isadora and Acacia were present along with Mavis and Jemima, though the former pair hovered at a distance and didn't look as if they'd actually participated in the battle.

"Let's get the rest of these beasties into our trap." Perry ran past, and a ghast went sailing overhead before crashing into the sage circle on top of its companions. It was getting pretty crowded in there, though the Wardens had set up the circle to cover a large section of the path.

With Mum's encouragement, the coven members began to converge on the circle and the Head Witches lifted their sceptres. Together, we cast the first banishment spell, and a handful of ghasts vanished into the darkness. We repeated the motion, and the sense of solidarity amid our group temporarily pushed aside my lingering worry that Linnea might return at any instant.

When the last beast had vanished, Maura turned back towards the coven headquarters. "I'd better set those council members free. Why'd she attack them and not the rest of the coven?"

"At a guess, she hoped she was taking the most powerful witches out of the picture." Unfortunately—both for her and the council in question—the higher ranked coven members were not chosen for their prowess in magical combat, and poor Chloe had just been in the wrong place at the wrong time.

I followed Maura's lead into the building, and she strode

towards the council meeting room. Without preamble, she opened the door to a room shrouded in darkness.

"You'd better stay back," she warned, stepping into the room.

I didn't see what she did, but after a few short seconds, the darkness melted away, revealing the table and chairs where everyone on the council—not to mention my assistant—remained slumped in their seats, unconscious. Maura moved among them, muttering under her breath. "They'll be okay. They'll wake up soon, now that they're out of that place."

"Are you sure?" Worry fluttered inside my chest, particularly when I looked at Chloe. She hadn't done anything wrong except work as my assistant, and the knowledge that she'd taken the hit instead of me made guilt squirm inside my chest.

"What's going on?" Mum entered, releasing a stifled gasp when she saw the unconscious council members.

"They're unconscious, like you were." I took in a breath. "This might be a problem."

"Yes." Mum's voice was flinty. "It is."

The sound of voices from outside the lobby indicated that the rest of the coven also wanted an explanation. Mum beckoned me out of the room, where the witches immediately swarmed the pair of us, bombarding us with questions. The other Head Witches watched from behind, Acacia and Isadora wearing expressions that suggested they expected a thank you and possibly a medal for offering their help. I didn't have the energy to deal with Head Witch politics, not when I was less than convinced that Linnea was actually gone. Maura must have slipped away at some point, and I almost wished she'd taken me with her. Almost.

I left Mum to explain things to the coven and ducked out

of the building in search of Maura, finding the Wardens gathering around the door.

"Where is she?" asked Perry. "Where's Linnea?"

"She ran into the afterworld," I explained. "Both of them did. I don't know if Linnea really meant it about this being part of some bigger scheme of hers or if she was just bluffing because she knew we had the upper hand."

"Knowing her, the former," said Tam, who had his phone out. "I'll have to report this."

"It's not even over yet," Perry protested.

"Yes, it is," Maurice retorted. "The Reaper ran off."

"And the Henbanes?" I swivelled to the building next door and saw that the police had the place surrounded. "Ramsey—are they in there?"

"Must be." He lifted his wand. "We're going to break down the defences. They have some kind of barrier on the doors."

"I can help." Maura popped out of thin air, making me and several of the police officers jump.

"She's really gone," she said. "This is bizarre. And suspicious."

"Too easy, you think?"

"Way too easy." She shook her head. "It's like Linnea wasn't really committed to taking over the town, which I can kind of understand, but I don't know why she didn't summon the demons while she had the chance."

"Are you absolutely certain she isn't still lurking some-where, waiting to pounce when our backs are turned?"

"No," she said. "She might be hiding herself from me in the afterworld. I'll keep an eye out."

"No, you won't," Mart interjected. "I've had enough trauma for one day. We should go home."

"You didn't even get involved in the fight." Though I knew the presence of so much sage was bound to be tough for a ghost to be around. "Let me know if you find anything" I said to Maura. "I'm pretty sure I'm about to get dragged into cleaning up the mess in there."

Really, you'd think a fight to the near-death would exempt me from dealing with Tiffany Henbane, but it was hard to complain. I was back home, my family was safe, and Linnea had—for the time being—left Wildwood Heath alone.

We'd won the battle. Next, we'd win the war.

9

No rest for the wicked. Or for the Head Witch, apparently. The Wardens had taken it upon themselves to undo the binding spell Linnea had put on the town while Maura combed the afterworld for the elusive Reaper, which left it to me to help the distraught family members of our unconscious council members take them home to recover. Grandma helped by offering cheery reassurances that the afterworld really wasn't that bad once you got used to the dark, while the visiting Head Witches hung around looking reproachfully at me as if disappointed that they weren't getting the VIP treatment.

I refused point-blank to get dragged into any meetings without at least checking that our enemies weren't about to strike us from behind, though Rowan promised to personally stand guard outside her mother's office until the police had finished dealing with the Henbanes and came to haul Aunt Shannon back to jail.

There was a hitch. The instant I tried to leave the coven headquarters, Mum cornered me. "Robin. We have a problem."

"If it's to do with paperwork, it can wait."

"No." She pointed at the transparent glass covering the back door. "It's that."

I followed her gaze to the garden at the coven headquarters' rear. "I don't see anything."

"Look at the maze, Robin."

I obliged, walking outside onto the paved area at the back of the building. The coven's expansive lawns extended to a maze of hedges, and something was decidedly amiss. The fence dividing the maze from the neighbouring garden had vanished outright, and the opening in the hedges had also gone—there was no way into the maze except via the Henbane Coven's garden.

"I can't believe this." Indignation rose inside me. Tiffany Henbane had made no secret of her desire to claim the maze for her own, but that she'd sneak in and steal it while I was gone was an underhanded move even for her.

Tansy scampered into view, Radcliffe close behind her. "What's going on?"

"Tiffany." I gestured to the maze. "This won't stand. Has Ramsey managed to get into their headquarters yet?"

"Nope." Tansy hopped onto the fence, her tail wagging. "Want me to chase them out?"

"Better avoid that place." The maze, on the other hand, I could handle myself. "Can you check if they left any booby traps on the other side of the hedges?"

"Got it." Tansy scurried atop the fence until it ended at the hedges the Henbanes had so rudely claimed for their own. "I don't see anything. Looks like a rush job."

"Good." I approached the wall of hedges, assessing my options. Mum would throw a fit if I caused any damage to the maze itself, so I pointed the sceptre at the fence instead.

"Robin!" Mum shouted. "Don't you even think about it."

"What do you want me to do, blast my way into the

Henbanes' headquarters instead?" That did admittedly seem like an appealing option, but the sound of thumps from the front of their building told me that my brother was doing a stellar job of that on his own.

Screw this. I conjured a blast of wind that hit the fences head-on, causing them to collapse like a stack of dominoes. With the path clear, I jogged into the Henbanes' garden in time to see my brother and his officers making their way through the coven's lobby to the back door.

Naturally, Ramsey did not look overly thrilled at the property damage I'd left in my path. I thought I'd been positively restrained, really.

"Don't look at me like that," I said. "I didn't damage the hedges at all, see? Did you round up the coven?"

"Not all of them." He eyed the hedges at my back. "I think the ringleaders are hiding in there."

Unfortunately, the maze was no easier to access from this side than from ours. While the fence had gone, a wall of bristling thorns occupied the front of the hedges on the Henbanes' side, as if they'd sprung into existence in the past few minutes, which might well be true.

Time for another tactic. I lifted the sceptre carefully, this time taking aim at the hedges.

"Robin…" Ramsey's voice thrummed with tension. "Do *not* damage the—"

The hedges flew upward into the air as I cast a levitation spell. Several people shrieked, and I glimpsed a few figures crouching around the fountain in the now-exposed centre of the maze.

Ramsey and the others ran in at once, and I held the sceptre aloft to keep the hedges off the ground while the police moved swiftly, rounding up the interlopers and handcuffing them.

At Mum's prompting, I returned the hedges to their original position, though the fences were beyond salvaging. Luckily there wasn't anyone left in the Henbanes' headquarters to object. Everyone present in the building had knowingly harboured a bunch of criminals, and for that reason, Ramsey and his crew had rounded up the entire coven for questioning.

"Got everyone?" I walked towards my brother, surveying the subdued witches huddled before him and noting a certain pair of faces were markedly absent "Where's Tiffany? And Persephone?"

"Not here." He scowled. "Maybe the others will be willing to point us in their direction when they're behind bars."

Tiffany isn't here. Had she run off with Linnea? No, even she wouldn't willingly go into the afterworld, surely. I hardly believed I'd done so myself, and I'd been lucky to walk out alive after Maura let go of my hand. Tiffany was far too cowardly to take the risk herself. *Right?*

"Don't forget Aunt Shannon," I said to him. "She needs to go back to prison too. She's locked in her office."

"We'll come back for her," he said. "Once we've checked that the jail is ready for inmates."

I hadn't checked on Rowan yet, either, and she hadn't come downstairs since she'd assigned herself to watch Aunt Shannon—not even to watch the Henbane Coven's arrest.

I ran back to the coven headquarters, climbed the stairs, and tripped over a body at the top. *Rowan.*

"Rowan!" Alarm rose within me as I dropped to a crouch. My cousin lay flat on her back, her mouth slightly open, locked in a powerful freeze-frame spell. Her tarantula familiar, Ralph, poked her in the face with a hairy leg, uttering chittering noises of panic.

"Hang on." I lifted the sceptre and cast a reversal spell. "Rowan?"

She groaned then sprang to her feet with a curse. "My

sister! She came in here and got our mum out. I can't *believe* I forgot about her."

"Vanessa?"

I'd admittedly forgotten, too, that Rowan's older sister had been jailed alongside her mother. Vanessa was usually so enmeshed in her mother's endless scheming that she hardly seemed to have a personality of her own most of the time.

"Where do you think they went?" I asked.

"I don't know." Rowan lifted her arm to let Ralph climb up her sleeve. "Home, maybe. Or the forest. I wonder if that's where Linnea went—it didn't turn out that well for my mum or sister last time they got wrapped up in her schemes."

"And yet they didn't hesitate to join forces when she offered them a way out of jail."

Hands clenched, I climbed downstairs and dodged Mum's attempt to waylay me again.

"I need to find Aunt Shannon," I told her. "Vanessa broke her out of her office. They've both gone."

I knew she wanted me to deal with the Head Witches—or whatever explosion of paperwork had erupted inside my office during my absence—but with Ramsey and the police herding the Henbane Coven to jail, I'd have to take matters into my own hands if I wanted to stop Aunt Shannon from escaping justice again.

I sent Tansy ahead to scout my aunt's house and found her sitting triumphantly on the wall, Radcliffe at her side.

"Someone's inside," she announced. "Want me to jump in through the window?"

"Nah, I'll handle it." I kept my eyes peeled for more booby traps as I walked to the door and knocked.

Vanessa answered wearing an almost-convincing expression of vague confusion. "Can I help you?"

"Yes, you can surrender yourself to the police." I wouldn't be fooled by her act. "And tell your mother the same."

"My mother isn't here."

"Sure, she isn't." I tried to see behind her, but she side-stepped, blocking my line of sight. "What's the point in this? You can't possibly expect me to have forgotten you and your mother were arrested only a few days ago."

Her bland expression remained intact. Her acting skills were almost impressive—no doubt learned from her mother—but I had no patience for either of their games. When she didn't budge, I lifted the sceptre. Vanessa retreated, shrieking, as the purple gem ignited.

First, I cast a reversal spell, hitting a half-dozen booby trap spells that lay in my path. As I marched into the house, Vanessa tried unsuccessfully to block my path, clutching her wand in a trembling hand. "You can't barge into our house."

"This isn't even the first time I've had to." I lifted the sceptre and blew open the closed door to the living room.

Aunt Shannon stood on the other side, a wounded expression in her eyes. "I'm shocked, Robin, that you'd intrude upon my property like this."

"After what you did, you have some nerve coming back home as if nothing has changed." My fingers tightened around the sceptre. "As if you didn't try to steal *my* property for yourself. Did you forget the time I saved you and your daughters' lives from the same rogue Reaper you decided to ally with at the first opportunity?"

"I only wanted to keep my family safe, Robin," she said. "I would have thought you'd understand that."

"And taking my sceptre was part of that, was it?" I queried. "Or was it more like you'd hoped it would eventually start to obey your commands if you kept it in your possession long enough?"

The sceptre had already rejected her twice, but she just wouldn't let it go. Pity she couldn't apply that level of passion to helping the rest of us deal with Linnea and her legion of monsters.

"It was an act," she protested. "I thought you would be pleased that someone in your family had the sceptre—not the enemy. I was trying to keep it safe while I pretended to be on her side. *We're* on the same side."

"You didn't think I'd actually believe that, did you?" I said incredulously. "You and I are certainly *not* on the same side, and you've got more in common with Linnea than with me. The only reason you caved to her is because you couldn't talk her into treating you as an equal."

Her wounded expression intensified. "Maybe we haven't always seen things in the same way, Robin, but you have my full support."

"Yeah, sure I do." I shook my head. "You're coming with me to the police."

"Oh, I think your brother might be a bit distracted at the moment," she said blithely.

My hands curled into fists. "What did you do?"

"I did nothing," she said, all wide-eyed innocence. "Without your brother here, some of his fellow officers made unfortunate decisions."

I knew she was baiting me, but I hadn't been to the jail yet, and I didn't entirely trust her not to give me the slip if I tried to escort her and Vanessa there myself.

"You also made an unfortunate decision," I said. "I'll let you know when my brother's ready to take you to jail again."

I slammed the living room door in her face and backed out of the house, a chorus of birds pursuing me as the local wildlife reacted to my anger. With a wave of the sceptre, I cast a powerful locking spell that encompassed all the doors and windows of the house.

"I'll watch her," said Tansy. "She won't slither out of there this time."

"All right, but be careful." I said the same to Rowan, who'd watched the whole display with an expression of utmost satisfaction. "I don't believe for an instant she had any intention of handing the sceptre back."

Once the house was out of sight, I broke into a run, following the main street through the centre of town. The rest of Wildwood Heath had suffered little damage from the battle with Linnea's monsters, but there was a clear absence of the usual bustling activity in the cafés and shops. Hardly a soul was on the street—with one obvious exception. The street was blocked by my brother, his officers, and his newly recaptured prisoners. The doors to the police station were sealed closed and covered with what appeared to be a large number of thorns.

"They locked us out," my brother said indignantly.

"Who is 'they'?" I asked. "My aunt hinted that some of the other officers made questionable choices…?"

"We thought them missing," Seth said, looking furious. "Apparently not. This is the Henbane Coven's work."

"Tiffany?" *Is this where she's been hiding out?* "I'll help."

I lifted the sceptre and swept the thorns aside, clearing the path. The doors sprang open and revealed none other than Persephone Henbane, perched at the reception desk as if she owned the place.

A small shriek came from behind me. Julian, the neat-freak receptionist, looked outright horrified at the mess she'd made of his usually tidy desk.

"You?" I lifted the sceptre and stalked towards her. "This was a mistake."

Persephone was less of an annoyance than Tiffany, but as someone responsible for abetting murder, amongst other things, she more than deserved her place behind bars.

A handful of uniformed officers flanked her, though a

couple of them backed away or exchanged guilty looks when my brother and the others came in.

"Get them!" Persephone shouted.

"I don't think so." I cast a freeze-frame spell that caught every one of them in its path, including Persephone.

She sat frozen at the desk, her mouth half-open. The officers she'd seemingly recruited to her side had also halted mid-charge or mid-retreat, some holding wands in their hands. I recognised some of their faces, but my brother knew them better, and the hint of betrayal in his expression struck my heart. A heartbeat later, he was back in police officer mode, giving an order to the remaining officers.

"Bring them in," he said.

I employed the sceptre to ensure nobody tried to slip away in the process, and it wasn't until Persephone and her allies were behind bars that I undid the freeze-frame spell keeping them caged.

"Where's Tiffany?" I asked of her. "Where's she hiding?"

"Wouldn't you like to know?" Persephone smirked. "Make no mistake, this is only temporary, Robin. I'll be walking free again before you know it."

"Sure you will."

Her words kicked off a nagging doubt in the pit of my stomach. I knew we hadn't seen the last of Linnea—and that corralling all her allies into the same place might not be the best idea given that the jail had been her first stop after her assault on the town. But my brother refused to hear otherwise, and besides, it was up to me to ensure Linnea didn't get a second chance to strike.

In the meantime, I'd never let the sceptre out of my sight.

10

———

I could tell Mum still wanted me to spend the rest of the day catching up on paperwork or entertaining the visiting Head Witches, but once I'd finished helping my brother relocate the prisoners, the Wardens needed my help taking down the last of the magical barrier surrounding the town. Glad for the chance to get outside, I walked with them to the boundary of the forest, keeping my eyes open for any trace of the enemy.

"It should be safe to bring your father and his family back once the barrier is gone," Tam told me as I lifted my sceptre to join Perry and Farley in removing the shielding spell. Maurice and Callum kept watch, occasionally startling whenever Maura and Mart hopped out of the afterworld to update me on whether they'd seen any signs of Linnea. The answer, thus far, had been a resounding no.

I watched the last of the shielding spell fade away beneath the shimmering glow of my sceptre. "I think we're pushing our luck by leaving the shield down—it means she can bring in backup."

"I thought most of her backup came from the afterworld,"

said Perry. "And the sage barrier is intact. We made sure of that."

"Yeah, I don't think Linnea really touched it, except when those ghosts first attacked," I said. "And when Aunt Shannon and Vanessa made a break for it into the woods."

The pair of them were now thoroughly ensconced behind bars, and I had to admit that I'd feel more secure knowing Dad, Jessica, and the boys were on this side of the sage barrier around Wildwood Heath rather than in a distant hotel where I couldn't keep an eye on them.

"Linnea never did come looking for us," I murmured to Tansy. "She might never have asked anyone about the rest of my family at all. Strange."

"Not really," said Tansy. "Your mother's side of the family's the only part that matters to her. You know, what with her lifelong grudge and all."

"I never really saw the point in holding grudges. It must be exhausting."

Aunt Shannon was a prime example. I'd have been content to forget she existed altogether if not for her and Vanessa's incessant attempts to make life difficult for everyone else in the family.

I did need to talk to her again, though, if just to pry loose any details she might have picked up from Linnea about the enemy's next move and where Tiffany Henbane was hiding.

"Tiffany's bound to be in the area," I said to Tansy as we walked to meet the Wardens. "There's no way she'd run that far from her allies. Maybe Persephone Henbane will talk."

"Who cares?" Tansy said. "This isn't your job—it's the police's."

"I know," I conceded. "I just don't like how smug Persephone was when we locked her up. Maybe I should poke her with the sceptre. Or set Maura on her. A trip into the afterworld might make her think twice about defending Linnea."

"Ooh, are we interrogating someone?" Mart popped out of thin air. "I want to help. I can be very scary when I want to be."

"You're better at annoying people than terrifying them." Maura appeared next to him. "Sorry, Robin. I can't find anything in the afterworld. Either Linnea's hiding in the deep layers or she's not in there at all."

"No monsters either?"

"Apparently not."

"Weird," I said. "Ah. If you heard me, I don't actually expect you to interrogate anyone for me. Mostly because my brother wouldn't allow it."

"Nah, we barely got back on his good side," said Maura. "Anyway, we need to keep an eye out for our missing Reaper. In a remote place like this, there's so little actually *in* the afterworld that you'd think she'd stick out like a neon sign."

"So would the demons, right?" But I knew—with at least two dangerous individuals at large who had a history with demonic magic—it would be foolish to dismiss the possibility of the demons slipping past Maura's notice.

"It's perplexing," she admitted. "Maybe they've found some other hideout to lurk in until they're sure I'm gone. Joke's on them, because I don't have anywhere I have to be. I can stay here all week if need be."

"You don't have to," I protested. "Drew and your friends are probably worried about you, aren't they?"

"Oh, they are, but they're used to it," she said. "I doubt they'd want me to come home and then have to run off two minutes later to chase some demons, anyway."

"Yeah." The nagging sensation in the back of my mind refused to leave. "I don't know what to think. I'd suggest they're hiding in the Wildwood, but if you can sense the whole area through the afterworld, even that wouldn't slip your notice, would it?"

Her brow furrowed. "I'll freely admit there's a chance they might have evaded me using some trickery or other."

Linnea and Tiffany couldn't have evaded Maura's Reaper senses, could they? "The Wardens can help search, but they probably won't be able to stay here much longer. They're bringing Dad and his family back, and then they'll have to report in."

"And tell their bosses that Linnea slipped her leash," said Mart. "Pity for them. This is why I always hated the idea of being an official Reaper."

"Me too," Maura said. "The paperwork alone is worse than the ghosts."

"I can't decide whether to treat that as an insult or not," Mart said. "Oh, there are our Wardens."

Sure enough, Perry and the others approached us with Dad and the others following behind. The two kids bounded along, not put off in the least by the disruption, while Jessica and my father wore tired smiles.

When Dad reached us, he wrapped me in a hug. "Thanks for keeping us safe, Robin."

I forced a smile of my own, my insides squirming with inexplicable dread. It seemed premature to bring them home, to act as if this was over, but I managed to keep up the act for the sake of the kids until we got back to the cottage.

Once they were inside, I faced the Wardens, feeling my smile slip away. "You need to go back and report in with the others, right? Will you be allowed to come back and search for Linnea?"

"I hope so," said Tam, "but we'll have to go through the paperwork, and there's bound to be some issues since we omitted some of the facts in our initial update."

"Such as you losing that shiny instrument of yours," Maurice added, eyeing the sceptre. "And a whole pack of criminals running loose."

"That's really not the local Wardens' business, is it?" Perry said. "Knock it off, Maurice. You're just annoyed because she turned you into a statue—which was hilarious, by the way."

The vampire scowled.

Callum cleared his throat. "Anyway, our priority should be making it clear that Linnea *is* still out there. If we do that, there's no way they won't let us come back to search."

"Lucky for us." Farley barely looked more thrilled than the vampire did at the prospect of hunting down Linnea, but the Wardens were a little the worse for wear after standing on security duty outside my flat and Dad's hotel room all night and then fighting a gruelling battle.

"I hope Linnea waits a day to attack us, just to give you a break." I tried and failed to maintain a light tone.

The Wardens were expert enough at finding people or creatures that didn't want to be found, but if Linnea had even evaded a Reaper, would the Wardens stand a chance of finding her before she struck again?

"They'll need to keep an eye out for Tiffany Henbane too," I added. "She's not as dangerous as Linnea is, but she's a powerful witch with a history of summoning demons."

"Hardly the first we've dealt with," said Perry. "We'll find her."

"I'll let my brother know you're leaving," I offered, partly to avoid going back to the coven headquarters. Mum was either keeping the other Head Witches occupied or fending off coven members asking for explanations, and I didn't have the mental energy to deal with that—or with whatever explosion of paperwork had erupted inside my office during my absence.

Instead, I jogged back through the centre of town to the police station and found my brother inside his office, planted behind the desk as if he'd never been absent. Even Prickles the hedgehog was back—as it turned out, he'd been hiding inside a desk drawer for the past day and had reacted to my brother's return by panicking so much that Ramsey walked away with a dozen spines sticking out of his hand.

"The Wardens are off to report to their bosses," I told him. "They're going to ask if they can come back to help search the forest. Have you sent anyone out there yet?"

"Only to check on the sage barrier," he said. "Otherwise, it's been hard to get people to volunteer. For some reason, they're not all that keen to face a possible ambush from monsters that can appear out of thin air."

"Did you just make a joke?" Tansy hopped onto the desk, much to the annoyance of Prickles the hedgehog.

"No," Ramsey said distractedly. "We're short-staffed. I'm going to have to stay here late."

"You can't work until you drop."

"Speak for yourself," he said. "How much have you used that sceptre since you got back? Don't overdo it. You might need your energy later."

"I'm sorry, who are you again?"

Hell must have frozen over if my brother was nagging *me* about overdoing it, but he might have had a point. Yes, my use of the sceptre was partly out of need, but I couldn't deny that the fact I'd come so close to losing it forever was also on my mind.

"Can I come back here and talk to Aunt Shannon or Persephone Henbane tomorrow?" I asked.

"No."

"All right." I'd revisit that question in the morning if he was in a better mood. "See you later."

When I returned to the coven headquarters, I braced myself to check on my office for the first time since I'd returned. Once I'd closed the door behind me, I turned to my desk and groaned. "How has more paperwork appeared when the entire council has been AWOL for the past day?"

One of the many mysteries of the universe, apparently.

"What's with that face?" Grandma said. "Really, you should be happy. You have your sceptre and title back."

"I never lost the title." I rubbed my forehead. "Aren't you worried about Linnea vanishing without putting up a fight? And without summoning those demons?"

"No. I always thought she was a coward at heart."

Hmm.

Hearing voices outside, I ducked out of the office and found Mum in the process of herding the Head Witches out of the building as politely as she could manage.

"*Do* tell us if you ever need our help again!" said Isadora. "We would be happy to come back."

Acacia looked as if the next person to ask her to drive a pack of monsters out of town would find themselves turned into a flowering plant, though Jemima and Mavis both smiled encouragingly and told me to keep in touch. I had to admit it would be useful to have them in reserve if Linnea made a second power play—same as the Wardens.

When I was alone with Mum, she let out a faint sigh. "Honestly, Robin, you could have at least tried to make them comfortable while they were here."

"Wasn't the meeting room recently a black hole into the afterworld?" I said. "And the council's in a coma. Seems like that should be more of a priority than showering Isadora Feverfew with accolades."

"I rather hoped to convince her not to contact the press."

Ack. "There is that, but you know, we did nearly get overrun by criminals and monsters."

"Both of which have gone," she said. "Where are the Wardens?"

"They left," I replied. "After we took down the shielding spell and helped Dad and his family get back home."

"Are you sure that was wise?"

No.

Mum evidently shared my misgivings, but I could feel the energy that had sustained me throughout the day draining with every passing moment, and the mere prospect of another attack made me want to lie down for a nap there and then.

"The cottage has always been surrounded by sage," I replied. "It probably would have been safe for him to stay, in fact, given that Linnea seems interested in only one side of my family."

"It's lucky for them that she is," she said, "but she can easily remove the sage, as she did with the barrier around the town itself."

"Technically, that was Aunt Shannon." She was right, though, and that knowledge only fed into my sense of guilt and dread. "Look, if you know a barrier spell that can keep out a Reaper, I'll use it."

"There isn't one." Her lips twitched into a frown. "I asked your friend."

"Maura?"

That was a surprise given Mum's general distrust of our Reaper ally even before Linnea's betrayal.

"She's going to stay in town for a bit and keep an eye out for trouble in the afterworld," I said. "Linnea won't be able to slip past her notice."

I spoke mostly to reassure myself, since that nagging doubt had yet to go away—neither had my suspicion that the jail's newly rearrested occupants knew more about Linnea's true intentions than they'd let on.

For now, the workday was over, so to speak, so I sent out messages inviting the others to meet up at the Fox's Den. Within the hour, I found myself seated at a cosy table in the pub's corner with Rowan, Piper, Harvey, and Maura. Mart hovered at the end with a cocktail in hand—a fake one in a plastic glass supplied by his sister since he'd dropped the real deal one time too many. Ramsey had declined my invitation, but Radcliffe had come along too. Tansy didn't look unhappy about it either. In fact, the pair of them were sharing a bowl of nuts and taking turns swiping crumbs from under the table.

"You should have brought your camera." Harvey nudged me in the arm. "Captured this moment for posterity."

"What moment?" Tansy had heard him, though of course, he couldn't understand her.

"You two being all friendly." I wiggled my eyebrows. "Something I should know?"

Tansy flicked her tail in answer and sent a peanut flying at me, while Radcliffe ducked his head in embarrassment.

Despite the generally upbeat mood, I found my energy starting to flag as the evening progressed, and being surrounded by laughing faces brought an inexplicable sense of unreality—like the vision I'd seen through the Seeing Stone. Nothing had changed, yet everything had. But I'd come so close to losing everything that it was no wonder I felt out of sorts.

Maura and her brother left first. Maura had booked herself a hotel room—paying for an extra room in case Mart wrecked the place as he usually did—and while I'd insisted she didn't have to stay in town, it was nice to know that someone was on watch in case Linnea was lurking in the afterworld while we slept. Rowan left next, saying she needed to clean cobwebs out of her flat, and Piper departed soon after with the promise that she'd be back to help fix the coven's garden first thing in the morning. Then it was just the squirrels—and Harvey and me.

He took my hand underneath the table, lacing his fingers with mine. "Are you okay, Robin? You're being quiet."

I might have said I was just tired, but I had no reason to

hide anything from him. "It just feels as if we're pushing our luck by celebrating too soon. Is that weird?"

"Not in the least," he said. "After what you've been through, it's only natural that you're having trouble letting your guard down. But remember that the police are prepared in case anything happens again, and Maura's staying in town too."

"And we only have two enemies on the loose—not dozens." *Pity it's the most dangerous ones.* "I don't understand why Maura can't find them, but I'm sure they must be in the Wildwood. It's the obvious hiding place given how massive it is."

"Yeah, but her Reaper skills cover a wide area, don't they?" he asked. "Besides, Linnea is also half human. She can't live in the forest indefinitely. Tiffany either."

"She's been in a cell long enough that camping in the woods might be a luxury." It was possible that they'd fled the town outright, but that was more wishful thinking on my part. "Tiffany didn't even put up a fight. There's got to be a reason for that."

Aunt Shannon would know, I was sure, but I'd already put that on hold until the morning. Whatever my misgivings, I'd won us one night of peace.

Whatever waited on the other side, that had to be enough.

———

I knew when I woke up that something was wrong. I snapped awake, curled in Harvey's arms, when Tansy peered over my face and squeaked loudly.

"What?"

She squeaked again.

"I can't understand you."

Tansy let out a series of increasingly high-pitched

squeaks, each more agitated than the last, but I didn't understand a word.

"Robin?" said Harvey. "What's wrong?"

"I can't understand Tansy," I said. "Unless she's squeaking on purpose."

Tansy gave a squeak at such a high pitch that I had to cover my ears. More followed, and though she gestured wildly with her paws, not a word came through.

"Did someone put a spell on you?"

Tansy shook her head, her tail wagging. Then she hopped onto the windowsill, gesturing with her paws to tell me to open the window. I poked my head out, spying a pigeon perched on the roof. "What is it?"

Tansy shimmied out of the window and made a threatening motion towards the pigeon. The bird took flight in an incoherent shriek and a shower of feathers.

Harvey looked blearily at me from the bed. "I think she's trying to say that you can't understand other animals either. Right?"

Tansy nodded, squeaking with each nod for emphasis.

"What, someone put a spell on *me?*" How could that be possible? I'd been here all the time, and Tansy herself would have warned me if someone had got into the house. Unless they'd struck the previous day, when my guard was down.

Tansy jabbed her tail at my phone. I'd left it turned off all night, mostly to stop Mum and the others from hounding me while I was at Harvey's. When I switched it back on, the screen lit up with a dozen missed calls, almost all of which came from my mother.

"Mum." I hit the call button, and she picked up right away. "What is it?"

"Something is wrong with our family's magic," she said. "Come home at once."

"Is it to do with why I can't understand Tansy?" Had to be. "I'll be right there."

I ended the call and looked at Harvey. "I've got to go. I don't know what this is, but it has Linnea's name written all over it."

My heart broke every time I heard Tansy's desolate squeals, but no matter how hard I tried to understand, I couldn't make out a single word. My connection to her had vanished, together with my Wildwood magic.

Only one person could have been responsible. Linnea, it seemed, had made her next move.

11

I dressed as quickly as possible, then I ran back to my mother's house, occasionally stopping to try to speak to any animal I ran into. After I scared off a whole flock of pigeons, I gave up and sprinted the rest of the way.

At the house, I unlocked the front door and found Mum and Ramsey both waiting for me in the living room. Mum's ginger cat familiar, Horace, sat morosely in the doorway and meowed at me.

"I can't understand Tansy." I sat down, and Tansy perched on the armchair next to me, her head drooping. "Not a word. Has it affected our entire family?"

"It certainly seems so," Mum said to me. "All of our familiars are affected the same. Carmilla, too, though she's pretending to be asleep."

"Not just our familiars." I pointed in the general direction of the outdoors. "Every other animal I've tried to speak to has been the same. How is it possible?"

Tansy squeaked, flicking her tail towards the sceptre in my hand.

"This?" I held up the sceptre to eye level. "What about this?"

"The sceptre is still working." Ramsey eyed the purple gem gleaming on its end. "That means the spell, whatever it is, is only affecting our family's magic, not the sceptre. Nor our wands either."

"Well, yeah." I was sure even Linnea couldn't stop the sceptre from working, though given what she'd done so far, maybe I shouldn't make assumptions. "Have you spoken to Rowan? Or… or Aunt Shannon?"

His eyes narrowed. "Not yet, no."

"I'll message Rowan," I offered. "If you're sure it's the whole family that's being affected."

As for Aunt Shannon, she'd likely manipulate the situation for whatever it was worth, and it wasn't as though she had access to any animals in jail regardless. Still, someone must know what was going on. Someone other than Linnea, that is.

I sent Rowan a quick message and looked up when my brother began to walk towards the door. "Are you going to work?"

"I have to," he said. "I can't let this distract me from my job. I have a lot of catching up to do, to say nothing of everything Linnea ruined when she instigated her jailbreak."

"You know this is her work, don't you?" I gestured at Tansy, who squeaked piteously. "She's meddling with our magic. It has to be her."

"Obviously."

"And aren't you interested in finding out how?"

The answer was *yes*, presumably, but Ramsey always put work first, and he didn't rely on his own familiar quite as much as I did. "Fine. I'm going to wait for Rowan's reply, and then I'll come and speak to Aunt Shannon and Vanessa."

I expected an objection, but my brother merely shook his head in a resigned kind of way. "You know the risks."

Prickles the hedgehog followed him out the door. His familiar didn't look overly fussed by the sudden lack of understanding between them, but then again, the hedgehog's joyless expression was entirely normal.

Tansy was another story. Her ears drooped, her tail dragging on the ground in a way that made guilt tug at my chest. I'd never been cut off from my familiar before, and I hadn't expected to feel so utterly vulnerable and desolate. Tansy and I relied on each other so much more than a regular witch and their familiar did.

I would make Linnea pay for this.

Rowan replied to my message, confirming that she had the same issue communicating with her familiar and the various animals she kept in her flat. With that in mind, I followed my brother's path to the police station.

The lobby smelled strongly of disinfectant, and Julian was in the process of cleaning some nonexistent dust from the floor with a dustpan and brush.

"It smells like that Henbane witch," he said when I looked at him questioningly.

"You should be putting sage down on the floor, not sweeping it up." I caught up to Ramsey near his office door. "Can I go and talk to them now? Aunt Shannon and Vanessa, I mean?"

"Yes, but it's your funeral if they say anything you don't like," he said. "I tried to separate their cells so that they couldn't communicate with one another. Vanessa's is closest to the door."

"What happened to their familiars?" I asked, curiously.

"They're in isolation, too, away from their owners."

That meant there was a good chance neither of them had noticed anything was wrong, but if Linnea had dropped any hints of her plans in front of Aunt Shannon, she wouldn't waste an opportunity to gloat at me.

I whispered to Tansy not to say anything in front of either of them before I entered the jail. I made my way to Aunt Shannon's cell first. Ramsey must have conjured up an extra dozen cells to accommodate the Henbane Coven members there for questioning, to say nothing of his own officers, and they all watched with interest as I passed. I held my sceptre high, refusing to let them intimidate me.

Aunt Shannon sat on a bench in her cell, managing a decent level of composure despite her dull prison clothing. Her blond hair was neatly combed, and a smirk stood out on her face. "Here to beg me to solve your problems, are you, Robin?"

"Hardly begging," I said. "If you'd like to share anything Linnea told you, though, I'm all ears."

Tansy squeaked in agreement and then looked at me guiltily, remembering I'd asked her not to say anything. Not that it mattered, though Aunt Shannon's smile widened as she peered down at Tansy. "Poor thing. Must be devastating for her."

"Almost as bad as being locked in a cell." My hands curled into fists, and I hid them behind my back. While it might have been helpful that my erratic magic could no longer give away my temper, it was impossible to hide that I was seething with rage. "Same as your daughter. I wonder if she'll have second thoughts about letting you coerce her into helping you. Maybe she'll be willing to talk to me without you breathing down her neck."

"My daughter made her own decision," she said dismissively. "She won't talk."

"We'll see." I followed Tansy back towards the entrance, and we found Vanessa inside a cell identical to Aunt Shannon's.

Unlike her mother, she looked somewhat subdued, her hair bedraggled and resentment simmering in her eyes. "I don't need to listen to your gloating, Robin. Leave me alone."

"I'm not here to gloat—I'm here to ask some questions." I folded my arms. "Go on, we both know that I'm going to figure it out eventually. How did Linnea cut off our magic?"

"How should I know? I've been in a cage."

"If you don't know, your mother certainly does, but I think you do." I glared at her. "Did you and your mother help her stop us from accessing our family's magic?"

Aunt Shannon's derisive laughter sounded from down the hall.

Ignoring the stares from the other prisoners, I marched straight back to her cell. "What? Got something to say now, have you?"

"Only that you're looking in the wrong place." She gave another chuckle. "*We* didn't help Linnea do anything, Robin. *You* did."

"What the hell does that mean?"

She might be bluffing, of course, but she was obviously happy to sit here and play mind games all day, and Vanessa was equally willing to join in. I might have a little more luck if Maura came in to back me up, but I hadn't seen her that day yet, and I had less than an hour before Mum expected me to show my face at the office. I beckoned to Tansy, and we left the jail for the time being, Aunt Shannon's laughter ringing in our wake.

Ramsey didn't even look up from his desk when I entered his office. "Any luck?"

"You might show a little more interest," I said. "No, but Aunt Shannon thinks *I'm* responsible for whatever Linnea did to cut off our magic. She also finds the situation very amusing. Vanessa is singing the same tune as her mother, same as usual. Want me to take Maura and her brother in to encourage them to speak up?"

"That's really not something I can allow, Robin," he said. "I'll have a word with them myself when I'm done with this."

It looked like he was up to his elbows in paperwork for processing the Wildwood Heath's newest crop of criminals. I decided to leave him to it and headed for the inn, sending Maura a message on the way.

She came down to meet me in the lobby, her brother drifting along behind her. "Your magic isn't working?"

"My family's magic," I clarified. "Our ability to speak to and influence animals. I can't understand a word Tansy says, and the same is happening to everyone else."

"Weird," she said. "Has it ever happened before?"

"No, but Aunt Shannon pretty much admitted Linnea did it," I said. "She also said *I* was responsible, which I assume implies Linnea is still in the area though I drove her off."

"That, or she did something when she took your sceptre."

My heart missed a beat. "Oh no. Why didn't I think of that?"

"I don't know how the sceptre works any more than I understand your family's magic," she added. "But for the record, nothing weird showed up in the afterworld overnight. My brother or I would have noticed any intruders —Reapers or otherwise."

"All right." I grimaced when my phone buzzed. "Mum wants me to get to work. I can speak to my grandmother while I'm there. She's the one who understands our magic the best."

Not to mention it would be useful to know if whatever Linnea had done had affected the dead as well as the living. I was far from in the mood to go to the office at a time like this, but Grandma undeniably knew more about the sceptre and our family's history than anyone else. Whether she voluntarily shared that information until she felt like it was another matter, but this was an emergency.

I bought a latte and croissant from Were's My Coffee? on the way to cheer myself up. Tansy scampered alongside me and ate any crumbs I dropped, but guilt over our fractured bond continued to gnaw at me as I walked to the coven's headquarters and made for my office. Inside, Chloe's desk was starkly unoccupied, prompting another pang of guilt, though Carmilla lay snoozing in her usual spot in the sunlight streaming in through the window.

I put my coffee cup down on my desk. "Grandma, where are you?"

"Here, of course." Grandma popped up behind the desk. "I do hope you'll spend less time running off today and more time at your desk."

"Sorry to disappoint you." I gestured to her familiar. "Can you two understand one another?"

"She's sleeping, so no."

"That's not what I meant." I tried to summon up some patience. "Grandma, did you know our family magic isn't working? None of us can understand our familiars."

"Meow," said Camilla, opening one eye.

"She said you're disturbing her," said Grandma.

"Wait, you *can* understand her?"

Carmilla yawned in my face and then closed both eyes again. Her body language was easy to read, but if Grandma's powers were intact and ours weren't, I would have appreciated some clarity.

"Can you?" I pressed. "Because I'm not kidding, I can't understand Tansy."

"I can't understand a word that you young people say either."

"Grandma!" Exasperated, I took in a calming breath. "This is serious. Nobody in our family can understand our familiars. Me, Mum, Ramsey, even Rowan. Aunt Shannon and Vanessa hinted that Linnea was responsible, and I think she might have used the sceptre to do it."

"Well, *that* is nonsense," said Grandma. "Nobody who isn't the current wielder can use that sceptre."

"Is there another way she might have done it?" I asked. "How is it even possible to cut off someone's magic?"

"Nobody cut off your magic," Grandma said, as if I'd suggested the sky was purple. "Honestly. You should know better than that."

"Then what?" I asked. "I know our family's gift isn't the same as regular magic, the sort anyone can use with a wand, but I thought it was a part of us. And…" *Oh no.* "And linked to the Wildwood."

"Now the penny drops," she said. "Our power stems from the Wildwood itself, and clearly, the forest is fine. That sceptre of yours is tied to the same source, which ought to be clue enough."

"What?" My head spun. "Then… doesn't that mean it's only a matter of time before the sceptre loses all its power too?"

A moment passed.

"That is a possibility, yes."

Alarm blared. I turned my back to Grandma, ignoring her indignant huff, and left the office in search of Mum. When I knocked on her door, she answered after a short pause. "Robin, what is it?"

"What else?" I held up the sceptre. "Grandma just told me that the family magic is tied to the Wildwood and that the same source is responsible for the power that rests inside the sceptre. So it stands to reason that it's going to stop working at some point soon, doesn't it?"

Shushing me, she beckoned for me to enter the room. "Don't talk so loudly."

"What am I supposed to do?" I asked. "I spoke to Aunt Shannon, and she implied that *I'm* responsible for this. I wonder if she meant it was because of Linnea taking the sceptre, but I don't know how she can possibly have done anything with it."

"Neither do I." A moment passed. "However, I think it might be a good time for you to talk to the last member of the coven that created the sceptres."

"You think we should leave town? Now?"

"We don't have to leave," she said. "After you lost the sceptre, I contacted Adele Primrose myself. She agreed to come to see us, and while we don't need to recover the sceptre any longer, she's already staying in the area."

"You might have mentioned that earlier." Granted, we'd had plenty of visitors at the time, and now that Linnea's shielding spell was no longer preventing anyone from getting into the town, it should be easy for this Adele Primrose to come speak to us without any need to leave Wildwood Heath. Leaving was out of the question when Linnea was all but certainly hiding in the Wildwood itself and had seemingly even managed to tamper with the magic that lay within its winding paths. Magic that was supposed to be beyond access for anyone outside of my family.

I couldn't help thinking of that vision the Seeing Stone had shown me. Maybe I was close to seeing it play out for real. Or maybe it was as Mavis had said, and the future was shifting too rapidly for the Stone to grasp.

Whatever the case, it was time for me to meet the last surviving member of the coven that had created the sceptre.

12

Within the hour, Adele Primrose arrived in Wildwood Heath with a flourish of her sparkling silver wand. She was an older witch who looked unassuming enough despite the shower of glitter that accompanied her arrival, settling into her curly grey hair and upon her half-moon spectacles.

"You must be Robin," she said. "It's a pleasure to meet you. I am Adele Primrose."

"Nice to meet you too." I followed as Mum ushered her into the now-empty council meeting room, wondering if Grandma would make an appearance at some point. I wouldn't have thought she'd miss out on meeting the sole survivor from among the sceptre's creators.

"I'm glad you were able to get the sceptre back," said Adele Primrose. "Such an instrument is dangerous in the wrong hands, even if the person in question is unable to use the sceptre to its full extent."

"I know," I said. "The thing is… I don't know if my mum told you, but there's a chance Linnea might have meddled with the sceptre when she took it. She's done something that damaged my family's magic. We can no longer use our gift."

"Lady Wildwood did hint at something of that nature," she said. "Can you explain? I'm not familiar with your family's particular branch of magic."

"We can understand animals," I replied. "And command them too. The sceptre's power is supposed to be tied to the same source, so we're concerned it might stop working too."

"I see." She seemed to digest that for a second. "I would say that the more worrying aspect is that there is an enemy loose in your forest, especially one who seems to have evaded the attention of a Reaper."

"You really think she's in there, then?" My heart began to beat faster. "And… you don't know what exactly she did to affect our magical source?"

"I know the generalities about how a sceptre works, but not how it interacts with a family's gift," she said. "Yours is particularly singular, it seems, and Linnea's capabilities are also outside of my expertise."

"We need to find her, then," I said. "But I don't know how to find someone who can hide even from a Reaper."

"I thought your family claimed dominion over the entire forest," she said. "No corner is hidden to you, is it?"

"I don't think anyone in the family would claim to know every corner," I said. "But we definitely know it better than Linnea does."

Aunt Shannon might have told her the way around, but there was a limit to what she could convey without actually setting foot inside the forest herself.

"Then I'm sure you can find a way," said Adele Primrose. "I would act sooner rather than later if it's true that the sceptre's powers might diminish alongside your family's magic."

Alarm rose inside me, and I swivelled to Mum. Her

expression was impassive, though tension tightened her shoulders.

"Do you think I should find her?" I asked. "Before the sceptre stops working entirely?"

"Certainly not," she said. "Linnea will all but certainly be waiting to confront you."

"I know that, but it's that or wait for the sceptre to die and lose my chance. I don't have to go after her alone." But I had yet to hear from the Wardens, and I could imagine that Mum would be extremely reticent to take outsiders that close to our family's magical source. "Really, *do* you know whereabouts Linnea might have gone? I mean, is there a specific part of the forest where I'll find the source?"

Her jaw tensed. "Yes, and she cannot possibly know where it is. Nobody does, outside of our family."

"You and Grandma were waiting to tell me that, were you?" Panic gave way to anger. "You know what, I'll ask her myself."

I rose to my feet, waving goodbye to decorum, and I heard Mum apologising to our visitor as I sprinted from the room and all but slammed into my own office.

Carmilla woke with a disgruntled yowl. "What's with the racket?"

"The Wildwood is the source of our family's power," I said distractedly. "Linnea's in there meddling with it, and if we aren't careful, she'll cut off my access to the sceptre as well as my other powers. Grandma, do you have any idea how I can stop her?"

"You can start by going directly to the source, Robin." My grandmother floated into view from behind a cabinet. "Put that sceptre of yours to good use. It's worth twelve of that pathetic Reaper."

"Directly to the source?" I echoed. "And where exactly is that?"

"I told you to use the sceptre." She reached out and gave it a poke, causing the instrument to jump in my hands. "Really, you aren't *that* slow, Robin."

Right. If I used the sceptre to cast a tracking spell to take me to the source of its power, that *might* work—but at the risk of landing right next to Linnea too.

Then again, wasn't that exactly what I needed? To confront her alone, away from her army?

"There's no way Mum will let me go in there alone," I said, "but the Wardens are probably tied up with paperwork."

"Your Reaper friend isn't."

True, and maybe Maura would be willing to join me on a last-ditch attempt to find Linnea before she outright killed the sceptre's power.

"I'll ask her," I said. "But Linnea has somehow evaded her attention despite them both being Reapers. Any idea how that's possible?"

"Just because I spend longer in the afterworld than the average person does not make me an expert, Robin Wildwood," she said. "Any funny business from that Reaper of yours and I'll chase her off myself."

"She's not the Reaper I'm looking for." A half-hearted Star Wars reference that, predictably, sailed straight over her ghostly head. "Right, right. I'll ask her."

I sent a message to Maura and walked to meet her outside the café, where she stood sipping a latte.

"Does your mother mind you running away from the office every five minutes?" she asked.

"Yes, but we have a crisis on our hands." In brief, I told her what Grandma and Adele Primrose had said to me. "So with my family's magic source inside the forest itself and Linnea also in there, we're in serious trouble unless I go in and fix whatever she did. But not knowing where she's hiding is a major issue."

"Reaper trickery," Maura muttered. "She probably had more training than I did, before she went rogue. She's unlikely to be hiding *inside* the afterworld, though. Not if she wants to communicate with her human allies."

Tiffany. Right, she was in there too. "Can you track *her* through the afterworld?"

She blinked, considering this. "Usually I can only track people I've actually met."

Maybe not, then. "Tiffany was already in jail when you first came here. You never saw her."

"But *I* did." Mart appeared at her side. "When your delightful brother locked me up."

"And you immediately sneaked out again." *Wait a moment.* "You're a Reaper. Can *you* find Tiffany?"

"He *can*," Maura supplied. "But he won't without bribery. Usually letting him choose a film for movie night will do the trick."

"What movie night?"

"The one I've just invented," Mart informed me. "This weekend. Don't miss it."

"Does your sister mind staying in the town until the weekend just to watch a movie?"

Assuming we were even alive by the weekend, which was another question entirely.

"Oh, this is my idea of a holiday," Maura said. "I'm game."

"All right." To Mart, I said, "I'll let you choose the film for this weekend's movie night if you help us track down Tiffany Henbane. Deal?"

"Deal." He grinned. "It should be easy to find her given that she stinks of those awful herbs."

"Wait." I held up a hand as he made to vanish. "Not right now. The three of us can't go after her without any backup."

Tansy gave a loud, pointed squeak.

"Not you," I said to her. "Please, Tansy. It's too dangerous when I can't understand you."

She squeaked louder. Maura looked between us, her brow furrowing. "I bet she sounds the same to you now as she has to the rest of us all along."

"Yeah."

The sense of visceral wrongness persisted, and it was all I could do to resist the temptation to run straight into the forest, no matter the consequences. Anything to have my familiar back. "The sceptre can take me straight to the source, Grandma said, but if Linnea is there…"

"We'll lure her away," Maura decided. "First we'll find Tiffany. How long do you think you have until that thing stops working?"

I followed her gaze to the sceptre, my chest tightening. Maybe I was imagining it, but the gemstone on its end definitely seemed dimmer than it had before.

"Not long." I *knew* this was a bad idea, but if I lost the ability to use the sceptre, I could say goodbye to ever being able to banish those demons. "Mart, can you check where Tiffany is without letting her see you?"

"I am a master of stealth," he said. "It's no problem."

It is. "If Linnea is there…"

Maura caught my arm. "Don't, or else he'll have you strong-armed into suffering movie nights alongside him for the next year. It'll take him less than a second to find Tiffany. Linnea won't know."

I was less than convinced, but I nodded. Mart vanished. Between one blink and the next, he was back, a grin on his face. "She's wandering around alone, the silly thing. I think her Reaper friend ditched her."

"Huh." Maura's forehead scrunched up. "Are you sure?"

"I'd definitely have noticed her walking arm in arm with a murderous Reaper."

It wasn't totally uncharacteristic of Linnea to abandon her allies, and Tiffany was hardly on the same level as her, but something about the situation had 'trap' written all over it.

And yet. When I lifted the sceptre, the gem gave a notable flicker, like a lightbulb on the way out.

"Do you think we can jump on her from the afterworld and drag her away without Linnea being any the wiser?" I queried. "Or should I just go straight to the source and leave Tiffany alone?"

"Wait for Linnea to leave first," said Maura. "If Mart and I get the jump on Tiffany, Linnea will either come to her rescue or come to chase us off. Either works."

Tiffany was far less threatening on her own, admittedly, but my instinct told me that Linnea wouldn't easily be lured away from the source she was in the process of destroying—unless, that is, I went with Maura and Mart myself.

"I think she'll only react if I come with you." I crouched next to Tansy. "Wait here for me. Tell Mum, tell Ramsey where I went, however you can. We'll be back in a minute anyway, but just in case there's trouble…"

Tansy jumped onto my shoulder, squeaking at full volume. My heart ached, and tears pricked my eyes when her fluffy tail brushed my neck.

I have to do this. I raised an arm and let her jump to the ground before I turned to Maura. "Take me with you. If Linnea thinks all three of us are attacking Tiffany at once, she won't be able to resist showing up."

Then I can go to the source.

"Let's go." She held out a hand. Heart racing, I took it and let her pull me into the afterworld once more.

A familiar dread clutched me at the rush of darkness that consumed my vision. I tensed instinctively, gripping Maura's hand tighter.

"I won't leave you stuck in here this time—don't worry." She turned on the spot. "Mart, do your thing."

He floated ahead of us with a purposeful glide as if he could somehow make sense of the unbroken blackness around us. Soon a window in the dark opened, displaying a forest path almost as dark as the afterworld. Through it, I saw Tiffany Henbane walking alone, unaware of the three of us peering down at her.

The window widened, and the three of us leapt out, landing on the path behind her. I lifted the sceptre—and froze when Tiffany moved.

Or rather, someone else did—someone made entirely of darkness, staring out the back of Tiffany's head with flat black eyes.

"Hello, Robin." The demon spoke through Tiffany—or to be more accurate, through the back of her head. The sight was grotesque. "Fancy seeing you here again."

I stared for an instant then found my voice. "I already banished you once. I can do it again."

"Incorrect." Movement out of the corner of my eye prompted me to turn my head to see the window of darkness vanish together with Maura and Mart.

They'd left me alone with the demon—and Tiffany, if she was actually alive in there. My sceptre's flickering light barely penetrated the gloom, and when I pointed it at the demon, the flickering died to a shimmer.

"Too late, Robin," the demon crooned, and then lunged at me. I backed away, holding the sceptre aloft, willing the light not to go out.

A sudden bright flash sent the demon reeling away—not from the sceptre, but from the person who'd just popped out of the air. When my eyes adjusted to the glare, none other than Mum stood there, next to Ramsey. Rowan was with them, too, and she hurled a handful of sage at the demon that sent it further into retreat.

A second flash turned the forest into a blur, and once again, my vision fractured. A heartbeat later, I was no longer in the forest but outside the coven's headquarters. Mum, Rowan, and Ramsey lowered their wands, seemingly having cast transportation spells at the same instant.

"Whoa." I took a step back, disorientated, the sceptre dangling from my hands. When I peered at the gem on the end, I found the purple glow had dissipated entirely.

"It's lucky Maura came to warn us," Rowan said. "Are you okay?"

"Yes." *No. The sceptre's light is out.* I was too late. "Maura warned you? Really?"

"She and her brother told us where you were," she said. "She probably figured you could hold the demon off for a few seconds."

My throat closed. "I did. Barely."

We'd escaped, but at the cost of leaving the demon in the forest—along with its summoner. And now the sceptre was no longer working at all. Heart sinking, I tried a levitation spell, pointing it at a branch overhanging the path. Not so much as a spark stirred.

"No." I waved it again, more forcefully. "No. It's dead."

"I don't believe this, Robin." Mum took me aside, dismissing the others with a withering glare that sent even Maura and her brother into retreat. "You ran off alone? After what I told you?"

"I wasn't alone," I said. "I went with Maura and her brother. I thought Tiffany was by herself."

"That was an obvious mistake, Robin. How could you take such a risk?"

"Because my sceptre was on the brink of dying." My argument sounded feeble to my own ears. "And now it's dead, which means I can't use it against the demons *or* Linnea. How can any of us hope to beat them now?"

"Robin, did you ever think that sceptre alone would give you enough power to beat those demons?" she asked. "Especially when you insist on making impulsive decisions that endanger your life and the people around you?"

Her words lodged in my chest like thorns. Tears burned my eyes, all arguments turning to dust on my tongue. "Grandma said I should do it. She told me only the sceptre could find the source."

"Has my mother *ever* given you reason to think she was worth going to for advice?"

A fluffy tail tickled my ear as Tansy jumped up to comfort me. Even that didn't banish the awareness that I'd massively screwed up—and that Linnea would all but certainly move up the timeline of the inevitable attack she was planning.

"The enemy was in the forest all along," I pushed on, ineffectually. "We would have been forced into confronting her no matter what, and that's the truth. If anything, we should have acted sooner, *before* she summoned the demons."

"That was never an option," she said. "I wouldn't be surprised if she'd summoned them as soon as she thought she was losing yesterday's battle and kept them hidden for the opportune moment. In confronting them, you've put everyone in the town at risk."

Shame scorched my neck. She was right, and on top of the blow to my pride, I had to reckon with the knowledge that while the sceptre had chosen me as its wielder, that had been while it had functioned.

I'd been chosen as Head Witch to banish the demons, but with the sceptre no longer working, did I count as a Head Witch at all?

13

Mum finished her tirade, and Ramsey approached me next.

I rubbed my eyes. "Please don't say you agree with her. I already know."

"That's not what I was going to say." He looked almost as deflated as I felt. "Without the sceptre, we'll be hard-pressed to hold off the demons, even with the sage barriers between them and Wildwood Heath."

"That, and Linnea can walk straight through them." I'd got her attention now, and anything she did next would be my responsibility.

"Not if I keep watch," Maura said. She and her brother had hovered awkwardly in the background while Mum and I had our shouting match, and it probably said a lot about the seriousness of the situation that even Mart hadn't offered a flippant comment.

"What if she manages to stay hidden from you?" I asked. "You didn't know she summoned the demon either."

Maura scowled. "No, but if she comes near the sage

barrier, I won't need my Reaper senses to spot her. I assume the police will also be keeping watch?"

I looked questioningly at Ramsey, figuring he'd be displeased at her authoritative tone, but the only betrayal of his annoyance was a slight twitch in his jaw. "I already have patrols on the main forest paths, and they're in constant contact with me. If all of you could refrain from running into the forest alone while I'm not looking, I can update them on the current situation."

"That seemed like it was directed at one person in particular," Mart remarked as he walked away. "Was it me?"

"Mart, quit it," Maura muttered. "Robin, have you heard from the Wardens yet?"

"Nope." I got out my phone and sent a message to Perry, underlining the renewed urgency of the situation. I figured that telling them an attack was imminent might prompt them to ditch the paperwork for the time being, but from the way Mum was making not-so-subtle gestures from in front of the coven headquarters, I knew she wanted me to go back in there, possibly to apologise to Adele Primrose for being such a terrible host.

I did have a few more questions about the sceptre, so I resignedly ducked into the lobby and made for the meeting room.

Mum snagged my arm on the way past and whispered, "Tell her to leave, but do be polite about it. I'm going to put out word to the coven and ask who is willing to help us in the fight."

"I need to talk to her first," I said. "I have a few more questions."

"Very well." Her nostrils flared. "I'd better not come back to find you've gone again, Robin Wildwood."

"You won't." I'd learned *that* lesson, and the raw sting of her earlier comments pursued me into the meeting room.

Adele Primrose sat exactly where I'd left her, reading a book that vanished from her hand when I tried to read its cover.

"Your mother said you ran into the forest alone," she said. "I'm glad you're unhurt."

Heat crept up my neck. "I wasn't alone. I was with Maura, the Reaper. We tracked Linnea's human ally, but we didn't realise she was already possessed by a demon."

She raised a brow. "You banished it?"

"I couldn't." I held up the sceptre to display the gem on the end, now as lifeless and dull as a rock. "It's dead. Whatever Linnea did to the forest, she broke my sceptre as well as our family's magic."

"That's not possible," she said. "I've seen sceptres that were damaged, Robin, but yours is whole."

"But my magic isn't working." I frowned. "Isn't that essentially the same thing?"

"No." She rubbed her forehead. "I have to admit your case perplexes me. The sceptre itself is intact, but its power has undeniably been affected by Linnea's actions inside the forest."

"I know." Didn't mean I knew *how* she'd done it. "My mum and I did tell you the sceptre was supposedly tied to the same source. If that isn't true for other sceptres, how does it work for them?"

"The source is usually in here." She reached out a gnarled hand to point at the gem on the sceptre's end, her fingertip trailing down its wooden length. "All wands—and sceptres—are created by taking a piece of wood from a tree that has magical qualities and imbuing it with certain spells."

"A tree." Wait a moment. "Are you saying the source for this one came from the Wildwood?"

"It did," she confirmed. "That's the only way it can be possible that your sceptre's power source is both inside the instrument itself and in the forest at the same time. The two are intertwined."

"Have you spoken to my grandmother yet?" I asked curiously. "I would have thought she'd have stopped by."

"Lady Wildwood did mention her mother was still present in the building, but no, I haven't seen her."

Strange. Had Grandma been avoiding her out of her usual antisocial nature, or was there another reason? Regardless, between the two of them, they'd put together a picture that both made sense and made Linnea's presence in the forest even more alarming.

"So, Linnea meddled with the source in the forest and the effect passed on to the sceptre," I said slowly. "My grandmother said that I could find my way to the source using the sceptre, which is what I planned to do, but the light went out before I had the chance to see what Linnea did."

"I see." She pursed her lips. "It's possible, then, that the source inside the forest is still alive."

"Alive." Comprehension dawned. "You mean the tree that was originally used in its creation?"

"I would hazard a guess that that is true, yes," she said. "Your grandmother will know."

Yes. She would. And I needed to have words with her for another reason too. Unfortunately, since she hadn't deigned to acknowledge our guest and my mother wasn't around, I'd have to go back to my office again. "Ah, do you mind waiting for me in here? I'm sorry I keep running off. I know my mother thinks I'm the worst host on the planet."

I probably should have at least attempted to retain my dignity as Head Witch, but between the broken sceptre and the absolute mess that I'd already caused that day, I didn't have the energy left for pretence.

"Oh, I've seen far worse from Head Witches in the past," she remarked. "I've met enough of you."

Right, of course she has. I swallowed a sudden deluge of questions and ducked out of the room, hurrying back to my office.

"Grandma." I closed the door. "I need to talk to you."

My grandmother popped up behind the desk. "Good, you're alive."

"No thanks to you," I accused. "Linnea already summoned the demons, *and* she killed the sceptre."

"It doesn't look dead to me."

My gaze dropped to the sceptre. "In what way? And, for that matter, Adele Primrose just told me that the tree that was used to create the sceptre is still alive inside the forest. Is that true?"

"Isn't that what I told you?"

"Definitely not," I said firmly. "I'm assuming that most sceptres' original trees are *not* still alive. That's what Adele Primrose implied. If it's not working, doesn't that mean Linnea damaged the tree? Or—destroyed it?"

"That's not possible," she said. "The entire Wildwood would fall to pieces if she had."

"And you're absolutely sure that isn't going to happen?" I asked warily. "You know what, I don't want to know. If the source is intact—for the time being—I want to save it. If I can."

"Of course," she said. "Linnea might have infiltrated the forest, but she's not one of our family members. She doesn't understand the Wildwood."

Sometimes, it felt like I didn't either, but I *did* understand that I had to put this right. *Somehow.*

"Robin." Mum walked straight into my office without knocking. "You need to talk to the coven. I've sent out a message and asked for anyone who wishes to fight to step forward, but they'd appreciate hearing directly from the Head Witch."

"I don't have anything to say." Chloe was the one who usually helped me with that kind of thing, and besides, offering a motivational speech t a time like this might be beyond my acting skills. Luckily, at that moment, my phone buzzed with a long-overdue message. "It's the Wardens. They're coming back."

There followed a very confusing half-hour in which Mum and I had to escort Adele Primrose to an unoccupied room so that the meeting room would be free for the coven to use as a gathering spot. Mum went in there to give them instructions while I waited for the Wardens and prepared to explain my latest series of screwups and exactly what Linnea had been trying to achieve by escaping into the Wildwood.

Inevitably, explaining in full also required me to share a large number of my family's secrets that the others would have preferred to keep under wraps, but it was all but impossible to tell them why my sceptre was no longer functioning without revealing what Linnea had done—and why she'd targeted the forest in the first place.

"Damn," said Perry. "She did summon the demons yesterday? I should have figured she would."

"Her or Tiffany Henbane," I said. "I think we can safely say *she* won't last very long, but the demon is going to be looking for a new host after it gets bored with her, and we need to make sure Linnea doesn't sneak it past the sage barrier."

"Gotcha," said Perry. "You said there's already people keeping an eye on it, right?"

"My brother and his team, plus Maura and her brother," I confirmed. "The trouble is, Linnea's evading Maura's Reaper senses, and we don't know whereabouts the second demon is. They might attack from any direction."

"Your father and his family are back at home near the

forest," Tam observed. "Do you think Linnea might target them this time?"

"She might." They wouldn't be her priority, I knew, but the demons would certainly remember anyone they'd targeted in the past, and sending the Wardens to help evacuate them gave me a chance to look at the forest from the outside. As we walked to the cottage, I saw a distinct dark haze over the trees that hadn't been there before.

"The afterworld," said Maura, who'd come to keep watch outside Dad's cottage while we helped them get ready to leave. She, too, had noticed the strange, unnatural haze. "Even I'm having trouble seeing where I'm going in there."

"Are you sure you should be wandering on the wrong side of the sage barrier?" I asked.

"Linnea doesn't scare me," she said. "And I can't be possessed."

Maurice couldn't, either, but the rest of us were vulnerable. Including me. The demons no longer had any reason to fear the sceptre, and it was difficult to suppress the urge to step over the barrier myself to see how far the darkness stretched. How would I know if Linnea really had destroyed the source? *What if it's already too late?*

Dad and the others had picked up on my fear despite my best efforts, and this time, the two kids knew something was wrong. As we escorted them out of the forest, the two boys were both sobbing, though Tansy did her best to cheer them up while we walked to the inn. Her antics calmed them down, but I could see the worry in Jessica eyes as she coaxed the two boys to follow her inside.

"I'm sorry." I hugged Dad, my eyes stinging. "I wish I could have stopped this. I wish…"

"You can," he said. "Everyone's got your back, remember?"

"Or everyone's *on* my back." My phone gave a loud buzz

as if to prove my point. "Mum's after me again. I bet the whole coven's waiting for me to give them a pep talk."

It wasn't the coven. Rather, I found the four Head Witches, including Isadora and Acacia, waiting for me at the coven's headquarters.

I goggled at them. "What are you doing here?"

"Obviously, we're here to defend our fellow Head Witch," said Isadora airily. "And to ensure that the person who tried to destroy one of our sceptres is brought to justice."

My confusion deepened. "But… why?"

Quite apart from the fact that I was barely qualified as a Head Witch without my sceptre, they'd only turned up at the last possible moment the previous day and hadn't exactly been on the front lines in the battle against Linnea's monsters.

"Don't complain," Mum muttered out of the corner of her mouth. "It turns out that they're very protective of the one known surviving tree that was used to create a sceptre."

"You *told* them that?" Whatever had happened to secrecy? "Wait, did you know all along, like Grandma did?"

"I did." A hint of guilt entered her voice. "I should have told you, but I never would have guessed that Linnea would target the tree itself."

Indignation rose inside me, but I pushed it aside for the time being. I needed to save my energy for the upcoming fight. At Mum's prompting, I escorted the Head Witches into the meeting room to join a considerable number of Wildwood Coven members, some of whom I recognised, some I didn't. Chief among them were Piper and Rowan, both of whom waved at me as I joined my mother at the front.

The number of people present was heartening to see, even though I suspected that their arrival was due more to Mum's power of persuasion than any real loyalty to me. She'd always been better suited to the Head Witch role, and it had always been my hope that I'd be able to pass the sceptre on to her once I finished the task it had chosen me for.

With the sceptre no longer functioning, all bets were off, and I half-hid it behind my back while I spoke to the coven to avoid causing a panic when everyone saw the gem's usual glow had dimmed to a dull grey.

They almost *did* panic when the coven members and I reached the forest. The dark haze above had grown even more pronounced, the shadows blending the trees into an indistinct blur that even a Reaper would surely be hard-pressed to navigate. While Ramsey spoke to the coven, I took my mother aside.

"Is it just me, or is it looking even worse in there than it was earlier?" I whispered. "What if Linnea *is* killing the forest by attacking the source? If she carries on like this, the sceptre and our family's magic will never work again, will they?"

Tansy jumped onto my shoulder and let out a piteous squeak. The thought of never being able to understand her again… *no*. It was inconceivable.

"It's impossible to undo what she did without going directly to the source itself," Mum said. "That would entail you exposing yourself, Robin. I can't allow it."

"But what if she doesn't show her face until *after* she's destroyed the source?" Worry tightened around my chest. "What if that's her plan? She hasn't shown herself yet, even though she must know we're all here."

Tansy gave another distressed squeak. Mum said nothing, and my fear heightened. For most of our family, our actual magic was hardly the most useful ability we possessed. If anything, the others did their best to keep it on a leash. They spoke to their familiars but rarely bothered with any other animals, and they certainly didn't set swarms of birds loose on reporters who annoyed them. But the sceptre was another matter. Mum knew that, if nothing else.

"You know what this will mean," I pushed on. "Not only will I be unable to use the sceptre myself, neither will whoever takes my place. This will be the end of any Head Witches in our family, in our coven, in the Wildwood at all."

She exhaled. "I know."

"And I won't be able to banish the demons, but I realise you don't think I'm capable of that anyway."

A heartbeat's pause. "I didn't intend to imply that, Robin. What I meant was that banishing the demons permanently is out of the question, as it was for my mother. The most you can do is send them to a deeper level of the afterworld."

"Which is useless as long as there's a powerful Reaper who can just summon them back again," I said. "Listen, I'm not all that keen on the idea of walking straight into Linnea's trap, but if the forest's really on the brink of being utterly destroyed, there aren't going to be any second chances."

"No," she said. "If you want to do this… you don't need the sceptre to navigate the forest, you know."

"Come again?" I frowned. "Wait. Are you giving me permission to go back in there by myself?"

"You were correct in assuming that only those of us who belong to the Wildwood Coven are likely to be able to undo what Linnea did," she said. "And to do so will require someone to go directly to the source."

"Except that's what she'll be counting on," I surmised. "She'll be there waiting for me."

"Almost certainly."

"So, we either wait for the forest to die, or one of us sacrifices their own life. Not you," I added before she could speak. "I'm Head Witch. It has to be me. Though I don't quite get how to find the source without using the sceptre."

"With a finding spell, I'd assume," Maura said, looking slightly impressed. "You're really going to do this?"

"She certainly isn't." Ramsey walked over to us, a scowl on his face. "*I'll* find it. I'll take my team with me."

"Did *you* know that the source inside the sceptre is still alive?" I asked him. Based on the irritated expression on his face, I suspected Mum had only just dropped the bombshell on him too. "Never mind. You should stay on this side of the sage barrier. There's no other way to ensure nobody ends up possessed without us knowing."

In fact, the only way for me to guarantee that nobody who came with me into the forest ended up with an unwanted demonic passenger sharing their body was to go in with someone who couldn't be possessed at all. In other words, Maura.

Her and her brother's reaction to the news of the magical source inside the forest was as nonchalant as the Wardens' had been. Reapers saw weirder stuff than that on a daily basis, I'd bet.

Maura herself gave me a knowing look. "I can come with you. Can't promise there's much I can do to save this source of yours, but I can certainly keep Linnea's attention away from it."

"I'm not asking you to risk your life," I said. "It's more that I need someone get me out of there if things go south. Again."

Tansy squeaked, and I shook my head. "I know you can't be possessed either, Tansy, but I can't risk Linnea grabbing you."

"You think she'll be there?" asked Maura.

"I doubt she'll be anywhere else," I said. "But if I don't get her away from that source and undo what she did, there's no hope of getting rid of the demons. Ready to keep her busy?"

"Hell, yes." She cracked her knuckles. "I'm game."

"I'm not," said Mart. "There are demons in there."

"Linnea's more dangerous to you than they are," said Maura. "You can stay with Robin's familiar, then."

Tansy squeaked again, a sound that tugged at my heart-strings. I let her tail wrap around my ankle and stroked her with one hand. "I'm sorry. I'll come back for you."

And when I do, we'll be able to understand each other again. God, I hoped that was true.

Maura and I entered the Wildwood. At first, the path was clear despite the gloom, then several paces in, everything changed. Total blackness crept amongst the trees, and all sounds had been stifled.

Fear slithered down my spine. "It feels like she's close."

"Don't worry." Maura stepped forward without fear. "I'll know if she's near. You do your thing."

Easier said than done. I needed to get to the forest's heart, and again I wondered how exactly I was supposed to do that. For a finding spell to work, I needed to picture what I was looking for, and I hadn't a clue what the source actually looked like. A tree, I assumed—but that was not a helpful image to hold in mind when I was about to walk into a giant magical forest full of countless examples of exactly that.

Or is it? I conjured up a mental picture of the forest itself, the place I was always drawn back to, no matter how far I might travel from home. I held the image in my head and waved my wand.

The darkness vanished in a flash then came back with a vengeance as I landed somewhere awash in gloom so dense that I might have thought I stood in the afterworld if not for the solid path beneath my feet. I spun on the spot, squinting into the endless dark. Had I landed near the source? I didn't see any trees, but I couldn't even see my own hand in front of my face. All I could see was—

Linnea's smiling face in the darkness and countless monstrous shapes stirring in the gloom behind her.

"Were you trying to find the source of your family's magic?" she asked. "It's too late for that, Robin. The source is dead, and you'll soon join it yourself."

14

I stared at Linnea for a moment, then I shook my head. "No. I don't believe you."

The source of our family's power couldn't be dead. It *couldn't* be. I'd know. Tansy would, too, and so would my other family members. *Right?*

Linnea's grin widened, and it hit me how very alone I was. Maura was nowhere to be seen, and I'd purposely left the others behind to avoid them being exposed to the demons. But if I was too late...

"It's over for you, Robin Wildwood."

At Linnea's back, the darkness solidified, sprouting claws and teeth and all kinds of nasty appendages. I glimpsed Maura then, a pained expression on her face as Linnea's monsters surrounded her. *Why didn't I see that coming?*

I lifted my wand, but the light it cast was a pale reflection of the sceptre's usual glow. All I had left was regular magic—not my Wildwood powers.

I might never have access to that magic again.

No. I wouldn't accept that. The Wildwood wasn't dead. Even if Linnea had brought the afterworld itself into the forest, there had to be a way back to the source. But Maura was a tad preoccupied at the moment, and with nobody else to create a diversion, Linnea would strike me dead in a heartbeat.

My eyes locked with Maura's, and she shook her head a little. An indication to leave, to get the hell out of here—even if it meant losing her own life to the monsters of the afterworld.

I'm sorry.

I cast a transportation spell, and as I vanished, Linnea's voice lingered in my ear. "Run away if you like, Robin. It doesn't matter. I'll find you soon enough… once I've finished with your Reaper friend."

Then the forest was gone, replaced with the far more comforting sight of the road outside my family's house. At least, it would have been comforting if not for the darkness creeping around the back, casting a dense shadow over the rooftops.

The others were exactly where I'd left them, near the forest's boundary, and my appearance caused quite a stir. A dozen questions flew at me, all drowned out by a high-pitched squeak from Tansy when she jumped onto my shoulder.

"I'm sorry," I whispered to her. "I couldn't do it, and now she has Maura."

We'd lost the sole member of our group capable of avoiding possession. Except for Maurice, and there was no way in hell *he'd* risk his neck by going into the forest with me alone.

I approached the Wardens anyway, but Ramsey came jogging to block my path.

"We have a problem," he said, without giving me the chance to speak first. "The officers at the station aren't answering calls. I think something's happened over there."

"Like what?" *The demons?* No way. "Wasn't the place covered in sage?"

Unless… was this part of Linnea's plan too?

"I can't reach Julian," he added. "I'm going to have to go and check on him."

"Are you sure someone isn't trying to lure us away from the forest?" I asked. "We'd know if there were a demon in town."

Or Maura would—but Linnea had her captive, and she'd proven capable of evading Maura's Reaper senses already. Who was to say the demons hadn't done the same? Besides, Maura herself hadn't been inside the police station since we'd recaptured Linnea's allies. She hadn't personally checked that none of them were possessed before they were brought in.

"I wouldn't count on it." Ramsey eyed the Wardens, who'd positioned themselves near the main path into the forest. "You stay with them while I'm gone."

"Obviously, I'm coming with you, but I'll let them know." When Perry caught my eye, I walked over to their group.

"We think there's something going on at the police station," I explained. "Ramsey's calls aren't getting through, and since most of the officers are here…"

"You think Linnea prepared to strike from behind?" said Perry. "The thought did cross my mind. I was going by the assumption that Maura was right about the demon not being in the town."

"She's gone." Guilt tightened around my chest. "Last I saw, she was surrounded by Linnea's monsters. Better not tell her brother." *Not yet.* At this rate, we'd all be joining him before long.

My own brother was already walking away. I made to follow him and froze when a scream rang out from somewhere nearby.

A witch backed away from the trees, pointing at the blackness pressing at the forest's edges. "I saw someone!"

"There!" More hands pointed.

I squinted and made out an indistinct figure standing amid the darkened trees.

Tiffany. She didn't look overly concerned at being face-to-face with an army, but a glimpse of the flat darkness behind her eyes told me who was really at the wheel.

"What are you doing?" I called out. "Come here to stare at us until one of us gets annoyed enough to cross the barrier?"

She lifted her head, her mouth twitching into a cold smile. "What else? I've come to gather my coven."

A dozen spells flew overhead, causing my allies to scatter in all directions to avoid being hit. A second series of flashes ignited like fireworks as a group of newcomers ran into view, most dressed in the plain grey clothing of recent prisoners. I recognised Persephone Henbane among them, her mouth twisted in a grin as she took aim at a fleeing witch and turned her to stone.

"Stop them!" Mum shouted, and the coven witches shook off their surprise and turned to fight back.

The enemy might have sneaked up on us, but we had the advantage in numbers, and the air was soon thick with flying spells from both sides and the discordant snarls of angry shifters who'd come to lend a hand.

Tiffany watched the fight with a knowing smirk on her face, unable to cross the barrier.

"Don't tread on the sage!" I shouted at everyone within hearing distance, determined to keep it that way.

My shout drew Persephone Henbane's attention. She homed in on me and pointed her wand at my chest, but I cast a freeze-frame spell first. Without the sceptre's boost, she froze for only a heartbeat, but it was enough for me to dodge the spell she'd cast.

Not enough to give me an edge, though. Navigating the battle was a hell of a lot more fraught without the sceptre, though it did prove useful as both a shield and blunt instrument to use on any other Henbane witches who tried to get close.

Persephone's next spell flew wide as Tansy jumped on her arm, squeaking at full volume and then sinking her teeth into her outstretched hand. Persephone dropped her wand with a bellow of pain, and I cast a levitation spell to send it spinning away into the trees.

I'd lost sight of my brother, but when I turned my back on Persephone, I saw him duelling another Henbane witch some distance away. Someone had set the prisoners free—but who? Might one of them be possessed at this very instant?

"Ramsey!" I shouted to him when I was within hearing range. "Any of those witches might be possessed. We need to find out who."

"I can help," Perry answered. She produced a bag of sage from her pocket with her free hand. A flick of her wand sent a flurry of sage at an oncoming witch who had the misfortune to run straight into Tam's stick-like weapons.

The witch fell onto her back, out cold, but no telltale darkness rose from within her body. The demon hadn't possessed her, but how were we supposed to tell which attacker had an unwanted hitchhiker?

Stepping over the body, I heard laughter from the forest and called to Tiffany, "What? Do you care to tell me who's working for you on the inside?"

"Wouldn't you like to know." She smirked. "You always underestimate me, Robin."

"You're old news," I snarled at her. "If you're alive in there and it's not the demon I'm talking to—I have to admit I can't tell the difference."

"Get her too!" Ramsey ran straight at the sage barrier and cast a spell that sent Tiffany flying sideways into a tree.

I winced at the impact. "Whoa." I'd rarely seen that much outright anger from my brother before, but now that I thought about it, the demon possessing her was probably the same one that had possessed *him* not long ago. "Don't cross the barrier!"

"I have it under control." With another a flick of his wand, Tiffany flew forward, straight into a circle of sage that Perry had swiftly conjured onto the path.

At once, the demon rose from her body in a flat black mass devoid of any form or features. Except for those dark, dark eyes, fixated on my brother.

"You've made a mistake there," the demon growled.

"I doubt it." Fury dripped from Ramsey's words. "Stay away from my family."

"Oh, we already have your family."

What? Ramsey was here, and so was Mum, but… oh no. Who was left in the jail? Who hadn't come here along with the Henbane witches?

"Aunt Shannon." I spoke out of the corner of my mouth. "Or Vanessa. It's one of them."

The demon's cold laughter told me it had heard me, too, but I didn't care. If Aunt Shannon or her daughter were possessed and roaming around the town in search of victims while most of our defences were focused here on the forest, someone needed to find them.

"Whoa." Perry stepped away from the sage circle in which Tiffany lay. "I think she's dead."

"Is she?" She certainly lay very still, and she made no move to get out of the sage circle despite the demon no longer being in control of her body. "The demon isn't."

And I can't banish it. Not without the sceptre.

Ramsey turned his back on her. "I'm going to the jail."

"No—wait." I spun around when he turned away from the forest. "Ramsey! Don't you want to make sure that demon doesn't get out of the sage circle?"

"None of that matters if there's another demon roaming around." He picked up the pace, and I jogged faster, cursing the sceptre for being a dead weight but unwilling to let it go.

We burst into the police station and found the reception area markedly deserted. Julian had either run or gone chasing after the escapees, leaving a clear path to the jail and no obvious source of demonic presence.

"Careful!" I hissed at Ramsey. "At least get some sage."

Ramsey marched to the door at the back without speaking, and I followed him inside. While most of the cells were unoccupied, Vanessa still slumped inside hers, while we found Aunt Shannon seated exactly where we'd left her, wearing an expectant look on her face.

"I suppose you think I had something to do with those witches' escape?" she said.

"Obviously," I said. "The demon possessed you, didn't it?"

"Don't be ridiculous."

I sighed. "Can we skip this part? I know I've been speaking to a demon all along. You can't fool me."

"I'm hurt, Robin."

"Sure, you are." I rolled my eyes. "You've got her acting skills down, I'll give you that, but—"

A choked noise behind me made me spin on my heel. Ramsey stood with his eyes wide, frozen into a statue. But Aunt Shannon hadn't moved.

Instead, Vanessa pointed her wand at me next, the demon's eyes watching from her face. Vanessa. It had possessed *Vanessa...*

"Let her go!" Aunt Shannon shouted. "My daughter!"

"Hey!" I lifted my own wand to cast a spell, but Vanessa

moved with a demon's impossible speed, and my spell bounced off a cell door, leaving a dent where it had struck.

Aunt Shannon's hysterical screeches rang off the walls. "Let me out of here! I need to help my daughter!"

I ignored her and threw another spell at Vanessa. Again, she dodged it with a dizzying speed, and between one blink and the next, she had me backed against the wall, the demon's flat black eyes staring into mine.

"You're at my mercy now," the demon said softly. "The sceptre is no more. Your power is broken, Robin. The town is ours."

A red blur appeared in the corner of my eye, and Tansy jumped on Vanessa's head, her tail hanging in front of her eyes as she dug her claws in hard. Vanessa stumbled, yelling aloud in a voice that sounded much less demonic than it had beforehand. "Ow! Let go of me!"

At the same time, Aunt Shannon's cell door flew open, and she stepped out, her own eyes now flat black with the demon's presence.

"This one is a better host." She grabbed her daughter's wand from her hand and cast a spell that sent me flying backwards into the wall. My skull collided with solid stone, and my vision blurred into a haze of sparks.

My brother broke free of the spell and pointed his wand at her. Aunt Shannon flew back into her cell with a shriek, and the door slammed in her face.

I groaned, rubbing the back of my head. "Ow, that hurt. I'll get her back for that."

Tansy's squeak of agreement turned into a cry of warning. An instant later, Ramsey pointed his wand at me, the demon now staring from his eyes.

"Let him go!" I ducked the spell he cast at me then ran through the open door into the police station.

Another blast knocked me off my feet. I landed flat on my

back, right on top of something sharp that jabbed me right in the spine. I yelped, rolled to the side, and found myself looking into the aggrieved eyes of Prickles the hedgehog.

"Sorry!" I winced, rubbing my back. He responded with an inexplicable snuffling noise that I could only guess the meaning of.

"Your owner's possessed," I said. "What—*ow.*"

The hedgehog jabbed me in the leg and caused me to trip headlong over the threshold to Ramsey's office. I staggered, my head throbbing, as my brother came out of the jail.

"I have you trapped now," the demon said through his mouth. "It's almost *too* easy—"

My brother recoiled from the doorway, the darkness within his eyes visibly retreating.

I glanced at the floor and noticed the herbs scattered there. *Sage.* The office was surrounded by sage.

Prickles made another snuffling noise then jabbed his owner in the back of the knee.

Ramsey tripped, stumbling over the threshold to the room. The demon flew out of the back of his head as Ramsey caught his balance against the wall. My brother turned around, his eyes back to normal, and glared at the dark blur for an instant before it vanished like smoke.

"Get back here!" He made to follow it, but I caught his arm and pulled him back.

"Stay behind the sage," I warned. "You should have put it around the whole jail."

"It was Seth who put it there, not me." He narrowed his eyes at the spot where the demon had disappeared. "And I have a lot more of it."

The sound of the front door opening prompted me to peer out of the office. The Wardens came running in, with Tam leading the way.

"Watch out!" I warned. "The demon's somewhere in here."

"The other one escaped," said Tam. "The forest… you need to see it for yourself, but it's bad."

I swore, stepping over the threshold and into the lobby. "We need to cover this place in sage. The demon might be hiding."

"Got it." Ramsey ran out of the room behind me, holding a giant bag of sage with both hands. "I doubt the demon stuck around. How did you manage to let the other one escape?" He directed that question at the Wardens.

"We didn't *let* it escape," Perry said. "Seriously, that forest of yours is messed up."

"The forest?"

The Wildwood.

I ran out of the police station and made a beeline for the main road back to the coven headquarters. Already I could tell that something was terribly wrong. The darkness had spilled far beyond the forest, smothering the streets bordering its edges and casting all the houses in the vicinity in shadow.

Within the gloom, dark shapes stirred as ghasts and other monsters battled with the coven witches, who'd had the upper hand over the escaped prisoners not so long beforehand.

"See what I mean?" Perry said from behind me. "It's like the afterworld is… here."

"That can't be possible." I came to a disbelieving halt at the street's end. My mother's house had vanished outright, and even the coven headquarters was hard to make out through the haze that encompassed the street outside. "The sage barrier is still intact, isn't it? The monsters should be trapped on the other side, and so should that other demon."

"Clearly, they aren't," said Maurice. "You aren't that smart for a Head Witch, are you?"

"Knock it off," Callum said to him. "You don't have any more idea what's going on than the rest of us do."

No kidding. The Wardens spread out to join the fight while I lifted my wand and looked around for familiar faces. I glimpsed Mum fighting a ghost alongside the Head Witches while two more circled them from behind. I cast a freeze-frame spell on both, cursing its limited magic. The spell froze them only for a heartbeat, but luckily, Jemima was ready with the sceptre to cast a more powerful one.

Another chill brushed against my body from behind. I turned as Linnea appeared from the thickening darkness, her customary smile on her face.

I recoiled from her. "What did you do this time?"

"Nothing you aren't already aware of," she said. "Now that the forest is dead, there's nothing to stop me from taking your town, Robin. You've lost. It's over."

15

"No way."

She was lying about the forest, I was sure, but the afterworld had undeniably flowed over the boundaries and into Wildwood Heath itself. There was no escaping the demons now—or Linnea.

She gave her shark's grin and melted into the darkness. "You'll see."

I ran through the haze that now encompassed the road in front of the forest, eyes wide open in search of my family members. *Mum. Ramsey. Rowan...* they'd all been there, in front of the forest, when the afterworld had spread past the sage barrier.

And the demon had escaped. Was it possessing someone now? How could I possibly find them when I couldn't even see the ground beneath my feet?

Only Tansy's squeak of warning prevented me from running smack into a wall. To be specific, the wall of the coven headquarters. When the automatic doors slid open, I ran in, hoping the visibility would be better from the inside. No such luck, but Grandma must be around. I made my careful way across the shadowed lobby to my office, squinting through the gloom.

"Grandma?" I called out. "Are you in there?"

When I reached for the door handle, Grandma shouted, "Get out, fool! Run!"

I jumped. "Where are you hiding?"

"Here, Robin." The raspy voice that replied definitely did *not* belong to Grandma. A figure came into view, indistinct but unmistakeable. Adele Primrose.

The demon had possessed the sceptre's creator.

"Let her go," I warned. "Or I'll make you regret it."

"You can't pretend to be particularly attached to someone who was responsible for your dilemma, surely, Robin," said the demon. "If not for her, that useless sceptre would never have ended up in your hands."

"You're kidding me, right? Nobody deserves to have someone else hitching a ride in their body without their permission, especially a murderous demon."

"Pity." She lifted a hand. "This one is weaker than I'd have expected… but that sceptre of yours is equally obsolete, isn't it?"

"No." I lifted the sceptre regardless, as if it was more than a glorified stick. Its gemstone remained cold, dead. "Stop!"

Adele Primrose crumpled to the floor, and the demon rose from her body, its shadowy hands reaching for me. "You're next, Robin Wildwood."

I ran. I hated that I had to. Hated that I didn't have a choice but to run for my life, to flee like a coward right after seeing the demon kill someone who'd come to Wildwood Heath to offer me help. But without the sceptre working, I couldn't do anything but give up my own life.

I had to make it back to the source. And maybe, if Linnea was no longer there, I'd have a chance at undoing the damage.

I waved my wand, cast a transportation spell, and landed somewhere even darker than where I'd left. I might not have known I was in the forest if not for the fact that I tried to take a step and immediately tripped over a tree root.

I sprawled, groaning, and heard a familiar squeaking close to my head. "Tansy, you weren't supposed to come with me."

In answer, she licked my ear. *Not going anywhere. Huh.*

I pushed to my knees gingerly, taking careful shuffling steps to avoid tripping again. I pulled out my wand and cast a light spell, but unlike the sceptre, a regular light hadn't a hope of piercing the gloom. Had I reached the source? How would I know if I had? The sceptre's light remained dead, though I held the instrument out to feel my way around the area I'd landed in. A clearing, with trees around its edges.

I halted when the sceptre fetched up against a vast tree trunk. Cold energy rushed through my veins. I gasped, my fingers tingling as if with a static shock. I'd *felt* something stirring beneath the tree's surface—a kind of thrum like a beating heart.

The source. I'd felt it… through the sceptre. Was there life left inside the tree after all?

Tansy hopped onto my shoulder and squeaked a warning in my ear. I dragged my gaze from the tree and spied movement in the darkness near the vast tree trunk.

"Nice try, Robin." The demon's rasping voice came from the shadows. "I have to commend your persistence, but you must know there is no outrunning us."

"No," said the second demon's voice from the other side of me. "Now you're ours."

"Stop!" The word died in my throat as a numb sensation spread throughout my entire body from head to toe, as if I'd been hit by a high-strength paralysis spell. My fingers numbed around the sceptre, and though I could hear Tansy's squeaking, I couldn't turn my head to see her. Couldn't do anything at all.

Yet, strangely, the gloom was lifting, or at least fading a little, enabling me to see the clearing and the trees flanking its edges. A figure strode—well, glided—through its centre, her back to me.

Wait... that's me.

My body moved by itself, propelled by an unseen force holding it hostage. Dread clutched me as I looked down at my own transparent form. The demons had forced me out and had *stolen* my real body, leaving me stuck here as a ghost.

"Give that back!" I shouted, to no effect. "Get back here! That's my body!"

Was I a ghost now? Did it count as dying when I'd been forced out of my body against my will? I didn't know, but I flew after the retreating figure, not wanting to let it—me— out of my sight. But with the demon at the wheel and moving with its usual unnatural speed, my body vanished in a blink.

Worse, Tansy was nowhere to be seen. She must have followed, perhaps thinking I was still inside my body some- where, but I wasn't. I was here, and even if I technically wasn't dead, I would be soon. *What am I supposed to do now?*

My gaze snagged on something lying at my feet. The sceptre. The demon probably thought I wouldn't need it anymore, not now that it was of no use as a real magical weapon.

I crouched beside it, recalling how Grandma had lifted the sceptre during her first appearance as a ghost, but I hadn't really appreciated how hard it was to pick things up when you didn't have a physical form. My hands passed straight through the sceptre every time I tried.

"Robin?"

I looked for the speaker and spied a flicker of light. A person… or ghost. Another spirit, like me.

"Who's there?" I focused on the ghostly figure, and my heart sank when I recognised her as Adele Primrose. "I'm sorry."

"I was following the demon." She looked me over and her face fell. "It got you too?"

"I don't think I'm dead. The demon forced me out of my body." Though maybe the distinction didn't matter. "A Reaper would know."

Maura. Was she dead too? She'd been in a bad position when I'd last seen her, but Reapers were far more resilient than humans were. One touch from the demon, and my body and spirit had given up the ghost. Pun intended.

I reached down in another attempt to pick up the sceptre, which failed. Adele peered down at it. "At least the demons didn't get their hands on that."

"It's not even working." I swore when my hands slipped straight through the sceptre yet again. "Not that that would help when I can't pick it—"

The sceptre moved, rolling over on the spot. I startled, but it wasn't me who'd caused the movement. I lifted my head and saw more ghosts approaching from around the large tree that I could suddenly see with absolute clarity.

"Who are you?" The ghosts were too transparent for me to make out their features at first glance, but when I peered at the nearest, I gave a double-take. "Grandma?"

No, not my grandmother, but there was an undeniable similarity between their facial features. Behind her hovered several more ghosts, all witches, all with an eerily similar appearance.

"Who *are* you?" I asked.

"Who do you think?" asked the frontmost ghost, her eyes gleaming knowingly. "We know who *you* are, Robin."

"You're a Wildwood witch." I looked to the next witch, who was the spitting image of Mum. "But ghosts can't stick around that long, can they?"

Until Grandma, none of my relatives had died within my own lifetime, but there was little doubt that the array of witches before me were Wildwood witches.

"Yes, we can," said Grandma. "I told you so."

I turned to her, and this time there was no doubt that I was looking at my grandmother. She floated smugly beside Adele Primrose, whose presence near the Wildwoods only made the family resemblance even more obvious.

"You know them?" I gestured to the ghosts. "Did you know they were here?"

"Obviously."

The secret was hardly the biggest my grandmother had kept from me, but it would have been nice to know there were relatives of mine inside the Wildwood the whole time, watching out for me. "And you didn't mention it… why?"

"What use would that have done?" she said. "You didn't need more pressure on you. You had quite a big enough legacy to live up to already."

"Speak for yourself." My gaze panned across the array of ghostly figures, my nonexistent skin prickling. "Really, why *are* they still around? Is it to do with the Wildwood? The source of all our magic?"

"Yes," said Grandma. "Upon their death, each Head Witch can offer their own magical gift to strengthen the source, which enhances the sceptre's power too. The first Wildwood Head Witch began the tradition as she was unable to meet the demons' challenge alone, and the others continued to add their strength with each passing generation."

"Then…" I stared at her. "You didn't stay here because you wanted to?"

She hadn't stuck around out of stubbornness, but for the

same reason as the other Wildwood witches had stayed. Because no single person could beat those demons. These women had given their strength to their successors, one generation after another, in the hopes that one day someone would be able to break the cycle.

Now the task had come to me… and I'd failed.

Shame rose, so intense that I could have sworn my ghostly face was bright red. I averted my gaze from the others and spied a lone spirit in the corner of my vision. The witch peered from behind the vast tree, beckoning to me with a crooked finger. More to get away from the stares than anything, I followed her.

"So, you're the latest Wildwood." She had features similar to mine, and her face was surprisingly young. "I didn't expect this tradition to last so long, I admit."

"Were you… the first Head Witch?" I asked. "The first Wildwood to wield the sceptre, I mean?"

"I was," she confirmed. "I'm Violet Wildwood, and you're Robin. I've been watching over you for a long while, but especially since the sceptre chose you as its wielder. Or rather, *we* chose you."

"*You* chose me?" *Ack. Oh no.* "I… I'm sorry I lost the sceptre to Linnea."

I was sorry for a lot more than that, and somehow the idea that all my mistakes and mishaps had been witnessed by an audience of ghosts was more of an embarrassment than knowing the *living* coven members had been watching and judging me all the while. That I'd screwed up so deeply after they'd placed their faith in me to wield the sceptre made me want to shrivel up and evaporate on the spot.

"You got it back, didn't you?" She pointed down, where the sceptre had fallen from my hands. A flash of a red fluffy tail showed me Tansy crouched next to it. My familiar must have come back, realising I wasn't present in my body at all, but now she couldn't see *or* hear me.

"Tansy." My throat tightened. "I did screw up. Our magic, the source… is it broken?"

"If it was, we wouldn't still be here."

Oh. Right. If all these ghosts were tied to the source, it wasn't permanently broken at all. Not that I had any hope of fixing anything in the state I was in now.

"I can't do anything to help the source with the demon wandering around in my body," I murmured. "Can you help me?"

"We can't force the demon out of your body," she said, "but we *can* find that Reaper friend of yours."

"Maura." Hadn't she been surrounded by an army of monsters the last time I'd seen her? "Is she alive?"

"Reapers are made of strong stuff… not unlike yourself." Her gaze went to the sceptre, lying on the ground. Tansy trod around it, poking the gem with her tail and pushing her little paws underneath as if to pick it up. "I haven't seen a Wildwood witch with a red squirrel familiar for a while."

"Have there been others?" I asked curiously.

"Me." A wistful smile came over her. "My familiar was also a red squirrel."

"Oh." A pang hit me. "I guess she didn't stick around like you did."

"She'll be waiting for me, I'm sure," she said. "Whenever this business is finished."

"It's not going to be finished," said one of the other witches. "We've watched the same battle for generations. The demons just keep coming back."

"And we know whose fault it is," added another, who bore a startling resemblance to Aunt Shannon.

Violet held up her hands. "Really, you all made the choice, like I did."

"Some choice." Aunt Shannon's lookalike scoffed. "As if we all *wanted* to make our successors suffer for *your* mistakes."

"So you chose to stay," I surmised. "But it has to end somewhere, right? Don't you just need to banish the demons deep enough into the afterworld that they can't come back?"

"Nobody has ever managed to do so," said Violet. "We hoped, if enough of us loaned our power to the sceptre, one of us would eventually gain strength enough to do what the others could not."

"But you're stuck like this. This doesn't seem fair to anyone."

"Nobody ever said it was," said the ghost who looked like Aunt Shannon. "But the alternative is surrendering to those demons, and none of us are willing to give up the fight yet."

"Why *did* the demons come after you?" I asked of the witches as a collective. "I mean, it must have started for a reason."

"Because they want power." Violet Wildwood gestured at the tree. "We're brimming with it, and the sceptre terrifies and entrances them in equal measures. That's why none of us have ever wanted to let it go."

"I wanted to," I admitted. "But I guess that's not an option now, regardless."

"Oh, I meant giving up the sceptre's power in a different sense," she clarified. "The sceptre itself doesn't *have* to be in the hands of a Wildwood witch. I speak of something far more permanent… of giving its power back to the original source."

I thought this over. "What, putting the sceptre's power back into the tree?"

"Yes, and the same with ours too," she said. "It would be the only way for any of us to truly move on, but at the cost of depriving any future Wildwood witches of the chance to overcome the demons."

Oh. Now I saw their dilemma. "But… I mean, it hasn't been strong enough so far, has it? Even though all the wielders have been Wildwood witches, nobody has ever managed to permanently banish the demons. Have you ever tried anyone outside of the family?"

"There's nobody else who qualifies," someone else put in. "It's unheard of for that sceptre to *ever* be held by a non-Wildwood witch."

"Out of the question," another witch agreed.

Violet Wildwood tutted. "Some of the others have trouble telling the difference between tradition and necessity. There's no *good* reason to keep the sceptre in the family, and some of us would be more than happy to let it be laid to rest."

"Provided the demons don't come back." Which left us back at the first stage again. "How exactly does one get rid of them permanently? Isn't that more of a Reaper's job than a Head Witch's responsibility?"

"Even the Reapers have often had trouble with greater demons, and none has ever wielded a sceptre," said Violet. "On that note, I think some of the others have found your friend."

I followed her pointing finger and saw a pair of ghostly Wildwood witches floating into view, Maura walking between them. She looked a little disorientated, too, but her eyes widened when she saw me. "Oh no."

"I'm not dead." *Or am I?* A Reaper would certainly know. "Unless *you're* dead?"

"Much to Linnea's annoyance, I'm not." Anger flickered across her face. "And you're not dead, either. Where's your body—do you know?"

"The demons ran off with it. Literally." They'd have reached Wildwood Heath by now. My family might be interacting with me, not knowing it *wasn't* me but a demonic entity that wanted them dead. "I need to get back. Can you help?"

"Of course. Do you want me to carry the sceptre for you?"

"I…" I hesitated. I wanted my body back, but I hadn't fixed whatever spell Linnea had cast on the forest to damage the source, and the sceptre would be useless without it. "I need to undo what Linnea did to weaken the source, but I think I need my body to do that."

"No, you don't," said Violet. "You still have access to your gift in here."

"What?" I looked down with a yelp when she jabbed me in the chest, with the double confusion of her ghostly finger passing through my equally transparent body. "I can't use magic like this. I can't even touch a wand."

"Can't you?" She pointed at the tree with a faintly glowing hand. "Because if we're tied to the source, so are you."

"I don't…" I took in her glowing palm and then looked closer at the ghostly figures around us. Despite the dark, they also gave off the same faint glow. When I glanced down, a similar silvery sheen outlined my own ghostly skin. "How do I *use* it?"

"Like this." Grandma reached out, and the sceptre leapt off the ground, spun around, and planted itself in my ghostly hand.

Immediately the sceptre began to fall. I panicked, tightened my fingers around its edges, *willed* the sceptre to stay put.

This time, it worked. The sceptre floated in the air above my palm, as if I was holding it for real.

"But it's not… I mean, I can't use it."

Or could I? The sceptre's glow was starting to come back, fed by the glow of the surrounding ghosts. With each moment, it felt more solid in my grip, more *present*.

Bathed in its glow, the darkness began to recede. The trees became clearer, though washed out in the way they were when seen from the afterworld, and the sceptre's gem gleamed bright purple as if it had never gone out.

Tansy's triumphant squeak turned into words. "Way to go, Robin!"

"What?" My heart leapt. "Tansy! I can hear you!"

"Robin!" She jumped up onto my shoulder, wrapped her tail around my neck, and fell straight through my ghostly form. "You need your body back."

"I do." But I felt lighter in a way that went beyond my disembodied state. I'd regained my ability to use magic *and* understand my familiar. Even the former Head Witches were watching me with undisguised hope. Or pride, maybe, at least in the case of Violet Wildwood.

Elated, I found myself grinning as I waved goodbye and floated over to Maura. "Where'd the demons take my body?"

"I'll find them," she said. "Your familiar will have to make her way on the ground, but I'm sure those ancestors of yours will help her."

"You mean we're going through the afterworld." The dark, empty place was far less scary as a ghost, I'd admit. "All right."

We passed through the darkness, landing in an equally gloomy street that was somewhat more distinguishable with my newly adjusted vision. I could make out the flashes of spells within the general gloom—and then spied my own body, moving with purpose.

"Get out of my body!"

My body spun around—or rather, the demon did. "You shouldn't be here."

"But she is," Maura said and punched the demon in the face.

The blow was pretty impressive, and my body staggered

back, a dark haze spreading outward as one of the demons lost its grip and came flying out of me. *One* of the demons. Even with the blot of darkness outside of me, the blackness staring from my eyes was still present.

"Two of you possessed me at once? That's unfair." I lunged for the second demon and crashed headlong into a solid force that was both there and not. Darkness rippled around my body, preventing me from reaching it.

A pair of ghostly hands—*Grandma's*—grasped the rippling darkness. More hands joined hers, the other Wildwood witches having come to lend a hand—literally.

As the demon was yanked from my body, a lurching sensation tilted the world sideways.

The next thing I knew, I was back in my body. Dizziness swept over me, and I staggered, unused to wearing my own skin and unbalanced by the sudden heaviness of limbs I hadn't had for a while.

"Robin!" Maura held out the sceptre, and I gasped out a thanks as I lifted it from her hands. The instrument felt disarmingly heavy now that I was no longer a ghost, but the weight was a welcome relief. Now that I was back in the driver's seat, I wouldn't cede control to the demons again.

Linnea appeared from the gloom, her eyes widening as she took in the ghostly figures that had the demon surrounded. "What... how?"

"You should have checked that there wasn't anyone else in the afterworld when you left me for the demons," I said. "Really, you're a Reaper—you have no excuse for not seeing a few ghosts. But I guess that's your problem."

I lifted the sceptre, aware for the first time of the power of generations of Wildwoods thrumming inside it. Power that had passed to me. I would end this myself.

Linnea sidestepped and glided behind me with a Reaper's

effortless speed. Her eyes gleamed with malice as the two demons rose, one on each side of her. "Kill her."

"Why?" I lifted the sceptre, and the demons recoiled. "Seriously, *why* are you working with demons who can kill you as easily as anyone? The demons who killed your *family?*"

Her face twitched with anger. "None of your business."

"Since you wrecked my town and nearly killed me several times, I'd say I deserve to know the truth."

She lifted a hand. Darkness billowed out, but Maura got in the way. "Thought you could bury me under your monsters, did you?"

"Robin, watch out!" Tansy's shriek warned me that the demons had crept up on me again.

I turned on my heel. Twin pairs of dark eyes watched me, but I could still feel the power in the sceptre rising as the ghostly Wildwood Witches rose around me, each of them glowing with the same violet light that gleamed within the sceptre's gemstone. And within me too. When coupled with the afterworld already flowing through the waking world at Linnea's command, it felt almost natural to reach for that darkness and *pull* until a square door appeared in midair, similar to the ones I'd seen Maura open yet somehow... deeper. A fathomless pit, wide and yawning and ready to swallow the demons whole.

"No!" Linnea appeared in front of the window, barring the way. "They're mine."

"Yours?" Comprehension dawned. "You planned to turn against the demons all along?"

"They killed my family, Robin."

I gaped at her. "But... you tried to kill *me.* Even though I was literally chosen by the sceptre to get rid of them."

"You're hardly the first, from what your aunt told me."

"Aunt Shannon." I'd been right in assuming she was

responsible for telling Linnea how to get to the source, but even if she was aware that our ancestors were haunting the forest, she couldn't possibly know the full story, and neither did Linnea. "You wanted to use my power to banish the demons?"

"Not *your* power," she said. "The Wildwood. I wanted the source."

"You just hoped *you'd* be wielding it, not me." Who knew, maybe she *had* tried to claim the sceptre, and when it rejected her, she'd had to find a new approach to avenge herself upon the demons who had destroyed her coven and taken her mother's life. "But you nearly killed the source. Why do that when you needed its power?"

"I had to give you and the others an incentive, Robin. Your family members were incredibly reluctant to allow me to unleash my entire army against the demons."

"I can't imagine why that would be."

They wanted the demons gone, but on their own terms, not Linnea's, and they never would have wanted to endanger the entire village by allowing her to bring the afterworld to our doorstep. People had been hurt—killed—by what she had done.

"It's over now." She gestured towards the cowering demons. "Time to banish these creatures where nobody can ever follow them."

The door expanded, fuelled by the power of the sceptre and the darkness pouring from Linnea's hands. The demons shrank away from both of us, but they had nowhere to run. Linnea had brought the afterworld itself into the town and its surrounding woodland, leaving them with no hiding places and nowhere to flee.

Her plan had worked… but how many lives had she ruined in the process?

I lifted the sceptre with a surge of rage, and as its glow

brightened, the Wildwood ghosts moved even closer, their furious expressions mirroring my own.

"What—?" Linnea's eyes widened in alarm as a ghost gave her a firm shove, causing her to stagger several steps back.

"You didn't think the ghosts wouldn't have opinions of their own about you using their power, did you?" I asked.

"I suppose you thought they couldn't harm you," Maura put in. "Pity that."

The ghosts gave Linnea a collective shove, pushed her to the threshold of the door she'd opened herself. From behind, the demons waited in the depths of the void, eager to greet her.

With a cry, Linnea slipped over the edge. Her hands grasped the rim of the dark window as she tried to pull herself back in. "Robin. I—"

She was gone. Shapes watched from the darkness into which she'd fallen, their malevolent eyes inviting me to call them into this world to fulfil my every desire. The demons, too, lurked beneath the dark window, yearning to come back.

I lifted the sceptre, and with Maura's hands guiding the way, I closed the afterworld—sealed the deep hole in the world on the demons and Reaper both.

At once, the unnatural darkness began to fade. I staggered, stripped of that rush of energy. The sceptre's light was dying along with the darkness, and as the violet glow winked out, a sweeping black cloud carried me away.

16

I was back in the afterworld, where I floated for a while, unmoored. As my vision adjusted, I made out the Wildwood ghosts around me, though they seemed fainter than they had before, stripped of that vibrant glow. Hazy snippets of their conversations reached my ears.

"Time to move on…"

"No sense in staying now, is there?" That was definitely Violet's voice.

I drifted towards her, and when she saw me, she smiled. "Nicely done, Robin."

"You deserve some of the credit too," I said, gesturing at the fading transparent figures around us. "All of you."

Including Linnea, in fact, as little as I wanted to acknowledge her help. She'd been dangerous, erratic—fanatical, even. Her pursuit of revenge on my family had bordered on the irrational, especially as Grandma had never been in any way to blame for what had happened to her coven.

Really, Aunt Shannon was the person on whom she ought to have focused her ire, but my aunt had struck a deal with her instead. Perhaps my aunt had known that our mutual ancestors' power combined with Linnea's sheer persistence might be what was needed to end the demons' threat.

Oh, no—I'm not going to credit Aunt Shannon with any of this.

"Regardless, you did a stellar job," said Violet. "I'm proud of you, Robin. Don't forget that."

Her body turned more transparent then faded altogether, becoming one with the darkness. One by one, the other ghosts vanished too. With the mission fulfilled and the demons gone, there was no reason for them to stay any longer. They would finally be at peace.

As for me? Had I stuck around because I was supposed to hang around and give advice to the next Head Witch? Would there be a Head Witch at all, much less someone who needed to hear my expertise? With the demons no longer present, I wouldn't have thought it would be necessary, but I'd learned not to underestimate my family's propensity for keeping to tradition far beyond the bounds of reason and sense.

"Hey. Robin." The voice cut through the darkness. I squinted and saw Mart floating towards me, a grin on his face. "I knew I'd find you."

"What are you doing here?"

"Where else would I be? I'm dead." He gave a twirl on the spot. "*You* aren't, and my sister is quite insistent that you come with me."

I'm not dead. Bolstered, I followed his lead through the dark haze and spied Maura waiting ahead, a solid figure amid the blackness.

"There you are," she said. "I've been wandering in circles for ages. The entire afterworld got stirred up because of what Linnea did."

"And I got disconnected from my body again?"

"Pretty much," she said. "I can take you back, but I've never done it before, and I have no idea what I'm doing. Fair warning."

"You're not really selling this to me." But I had to make it back to my body if I wanted to see my friends and family again. I reached out hesitantly, and Maura took my hand.

She pulled me out of the darkness and into my own bedroom. Maura released me, and I spun in the air in disorientating circles, disarmed by the sight of my own body lying in bed below, pale and still, while my family and friends gathered around looking down at my sleeping body.

Mum, Ramsey, Rowan, and Piper. Harvey, too, with Tansy perched on his shoulder.

"Good luck." Maura gave me a firm shove and sent me tumbling head over heels, down towards my body.

With a jolt, I jerked upright in bed. My eyes flew open, and the sea of concerned expressions before me immediately morphed into shock.

As the world reorientated itself around me, Tansy leapt onto my head and shrieked, "You're alive!"

"I am," I croaked, my throat dry. "Just needed a bit of help coming back to the land of the living."

"I told you I could get her." Maura appeared at my bedside, addressing the others. "No problems."

"The last Reaper we trusted to bring her back to her body had malicious intentions," Ramsey said stiffly.

"Because she's the one who pulled me out of my body in the first place," I said hoarsely. "Linnea… she's gone. She turned against the demons—would you believe it?"

"They did kill her family," Maura said. "It never made much sense that she'd ally with them, but she played a long game."

"And she also killed a bunch of people in the process, so she's hardly hero material," added Rowan. "Unlike you, Robin. I'm glad you're back."

"Have I been here a while?" Judging by how starving I felt,

I'd say so. A thousand new questions crash-landed in my head. "Is the town back to normal?"

"More or less," Maura confirmed. "The Wardens and I drove off the monsters, and the effects of the afterworld vanished when Linnea did. That just left the regular cleanup."

"The coven and I spent days cleaning up the aftermath." Mum's lips pursed. "It's been difficult to avoid telling them about the sceptre, but I was waiting until you woke up."

"Huh." I followed her gaze to the wall where the sceptre had been placed on a shelf as if it was little more than a giant ornament. "Oh. That."

I explained everything in a piecemeal manner between firing questions at the others about everything I'd missed. A lot of meetings, apparently, along with an inordinate amount of cleaning and hauling people away in handcuffs. The remaining Henbane witches had been rounded up—the ones who'd survived, at any rate—and some had been transferred to another prison to avoid any further jailbreak efforts. Aunt Shannon and Vanessa were still in Wildwood Heath's jail and would be for the foreseeable future. I couldn't say they deserved any less.

I didn't yet know how to feel about the role they had played in all this. That Aunt Shannon had helped Linnea was undoubted, but in a weird roundabout way, she'd also helped me find my way to the solution. She must have known Linnea hadn't a hope of truly grasping the heart of the sceptres' power as long as our ancestors were there, watching over all of us.

That remined me. "Grandma is gone," I told Mum. "I assumed you probably knew."

"Yes." Her mouth tightened at the corners. "You'll have your office back."

"My office." I gestured to the sceptre. "I can hardly be Head Witch after this, can I?"

"You were chosen for the role."

My head throbbed. I wanted to close my eyes again. "Yes, but the sceptre can't choose anyone else now, can it?"

There was an awkward pause in which nobody seemed willing to meet my eyes.

"What?" I sat up, looked between them. "What date is it?"

"November the fifth," Mum answered promptly.

"I missed Samhain."

Not that it *mattered,* if the sceptre couldn't choose another Head Witch anyway, but according to the time-honoured tradition, there would be no ceremony until next year.

I fell back onto the pillow, defeat washing over me. After everything I'd done, even after fulfilling the Head Witches' mission, I was stuck with the title for the duration?

"We'll talk over our options later," Mum said. "Get your rest."

Tansy planted herself in the middle of my chest as if to emphasise her point.

"I'm resting," I said weakly. "Not like I have much choice."

But I *did* have a choice about whether to continue being Head Witch. And with the sceptre out of the equation, I'd find a way forward. One that didn't involve giving up my own future.

———

I brought Chloe on board as soon as I went back to the office. She and the council had woken while I'd been out cold and were none the worse for wear for their ordeal in the afterworld. It was weird going into my office to find my assistant back behind her desk, typing away at her laptop, but stranger was knowing that Grandma wouldn't pop up from behind a cabinet the way she used to. With her gone, I could arrange the office however I wanted without causing any tantrums, but oddly enough, I had no desire to do so.

I did see Carmilla sleeping on Chloe's desk, but when I reached out to stroke her, Chloe whispered. "Better not. She clawed me when I tried."

"Okay." I withdrew my hand. "How're things here? How many miles of paperwork do I have to look forward to?"

She winced. "A fair bit. I had to stash some of it in a spare room."

And my desk was already piled high. I smothered a sigh and sat down. "All right. What do you want to do, deal with all this, or help me find a loophole in the rulebook that will let me give up the sceptre to another person without actually letting the sceptre itself make the choice?"

Chloe dropped her gaze to her laptop, a flush rising to her cheeks. "I looked into it. There isn't one."

"What?" I jumped to my feet again. "I can't be Head Witch *forever*. Someone has to find another method to choose who holds the title, or else just not have a Head Witch at all."

"That's usually what happens in these cases," she said apologetically. "I mean, it's not that common, but if a sceptre is broken or lost, that's it. No more Head Witch."

"Huh." I considered this. "I can say there's no more Head Witch, and that's it?"

"You *can*, but it depends how much of a scandal you want to cause," she said. "Also, well, the paperwork isn't going to go away."

"Clearly." I prodded the topmost page with a fingertip. "Surely we can designate some of this to the coven leader."

"Yes, but you should probably tell your mother first."

"Yeah." While it might be tempting to make the decision without any furore, I didn't want to leave Mum saddled with the burden of the paperwork of two roles at once without at least forewarning her.

I walked straight to Mum's office and knocked. "It's me."

"Robin." She barely glanced up from her desk when I walked in. "You've come to collect your paperwork?"

My jaw dropped when she indicated another neat stack next to her desk. "That's mine too? No. It's too much."

"Chloe and I will help you," she said. "Of course, there's a council meeting this afternoon, and you'll have to call the other Head Witches soon too. You'll all need to consult on how best to alter the rules of your succession given the new developments."

"Given that the sceptre doesn't work and can't choose my successor, I'd say I need to do a little more than tweak a few rules," I said. "More like throw out the rulebook entirely."

"It's possible," she said, "that if we go directly to the source, then the forest will be able to aid us in the decision-making process."

"You want the *tree* to choose a Head Witch." I released a disbelieving laugh. "How is that any more reliable than letting a stick make the decision? Whoever said that there has to be a Head Witch in this region at all, for that matter?"

"Robin." She sounded scandalised. "You can't abolish the title of Head Witch."

"Technically, I can." I wouldn't go that far, but I had to make her see sense. "I'm not going to do that, but I'm not going to stay in a role for the next year when it isn't necessary. The *only* reason I was chosen was to help banish the demons."

"No, you were chosen as worthy of the title by our ancestors," she said. "The other coven members and Head Witches will honour that and would be happy to allow you to work out another way of deciding on the next person to hold the title when the time comes."

"Why not just vote on someone, then?" I asked. "Like the

coven chooses their leader? It'd be a lot better that way. No potential for surprises."

"The whole point—"

"Says who?" I cut in. "I *met* my ancestors. Not all of them seemed that happy about the arrangement either. They only stayed because they believed that someday someone would bring an end to it. With the demons gone, there's no reason to force our descendants to be saddled with the same problems as ours."

"There has always been a Head Witch in Wildwood Heath," she said. "It's vital for us to keep the peace in the Wildwood and to protect the village as a collective."

"You can do that without wielding a sceptre," I said. "Haven't all the fights in our family history revolved around who got to hold it next? Even between you and your sister."

"Do not speak to me of my sister," she said. "She's lucky that her alliance with Linnea didn't backfire in her face."

Ouch. Maybe she still had some complicated feelings on the matter, but I did have to acknowledge that Aunt Shannon's absence from the proceedings would make the handover process much more straightforward. "Listen, even the sceptre's first wielder, Violet, never wanted this to go on forever. She's been stuck there for hundreds of years, waiting for someone to break the curse—and it *was* a curse, Mum. You should know that."

"And you want to render her sacrifice meaningless?" she asked. "Really, Robin, you should want to honour her, and all the Head Witches that followed after."

"I honoured them all when I helped banish the demons— you know that," I snapped. "What more do you want from me?"

"You've done more than enough," she said, "but you can't possibly expect to just step aside without any pushback."

"You're not just pushing back, you're dismissing me

outright," I retaliated. "I'm *offering you my title.* I don't want it. That's the truth of it."

Mum's mouth parted. "You're offering the title to *me?*"

"It's obvious the sceptre should have chosen you," I said impatiently. "I don't know why it skipped a generation. Blame Violet Wildwood if you must, but you're the coven leader, and why shouldn't you hold the Head Witch title too?"

"I wasn't chosen," she said. "It's—"

"Tradition," I finished. "I know. And I'll happily go through whatever ridiculous ceremony you like if you let me do it sooner than next Samhain. I can't put my life on hold for another year, Mum. Please."

She studied my face. "You really want to leave."

"I don't know what I want," I said heatedly. "But I haven't been allowed a say over my own future since I came back here. I'd say I've earned that much, don't you?"

That, and I hadn't wanted to think beyond the demons. They'd seemed such an unmovable force that the notion of my own survival had seemed shaky, to say the least, and I hadn't dared think of what might await on the other side.

But now that I'd won, the future was open, and… I didn't even know what to do with it, to be perfectly honest, but I refused to give up fighting for control of my own life.

"I'm sorry, Robin," she said softly. "I wish I could make this easier for you."

"You can," I said. "The point is that we both *have* the choice, and the other Head Witches never did. Even Grandma didn't want to end up stuck in that forest forever."

"No," she said. "I never got to say goodbye to her."

Regret rose inside me, unexpectedly. "I'm sorry. She was a great help to me in the end. She really came through for us."

So had the other Wildwoods, and while I wanted to

honour them, Violet had made it clear that I could do exactly that just by living my own life. As me, not as Head Witch.

"I wish I could have met the others too," Mum said.

"You never did?" I supposed Grandma wouldn't have had any reason to take her to meet them, not when Mum hadn't been chosen by the sceptre herself. "I can tell you more about them. Ramsey too."

"Yes, later." She turned back to her desk, her composure back in place. "I'll hold the paperwork here until we've ascertained the future of the Head Witch role. None of it is urgent."

I'd won one small victory. "And at the meeting, you won't shoot me down if I bring up hosting a ceremony to vote on the next Head Witch within the next week?"

"No." A moment passed. "We'll see if the other council members agree."

———

Some of them did. Others—not so much, but enough voted in favour for me to confirm the ceremony would be held one week from our initial meeting. That gave me time to clear the paperwork off my desk, fill in the other Head Witches on my decision—and more importantly, recover from the time I'd spent in the afterworld by spending as much time as possible with the people I loved.

For a few days, things went back to normal, or as normal as they'd ever been when I held the Head Witch title. I went to work, stopped by the café at lunchtime, and spent the weekend either with Harvey or gaming with Rowan. I hung out with Piper in the garden while she trimmed Mum's rosebushes. I watched movies with Ramsey when both of us were home at night. I even did as Mum suggested and told them in detail about my encounter with the past Wildwood witches, especially Violet and her familiar.

"I hope they found their way back to each other," I said to Tansy as we walked to the coven headquarters for the ceremony. We hadn't had many chances to talk alone that week, not just because of my own packed schedule but because Tansy seemed to have a full social calendar of her own—mostly revolving around introducing Radcliffe to her favourite haunts. He seemed intent on sticking around long-term, and as long as Tansy was happy, I was content to let them have their fun.

"They did," Tansy said with confidence. "Obviously, I'll follow *you* into the afterworld myself. Nobody will keep us apart, not even death."

"I bet you will."

She went scampering off to the coven's garden while I entered the building. As with the previous ceremony, the meeting room had been cleared out and the seats arranged so that they faced the front. That was about where similarities with the last time ended. There was no sceptre, for a start, and no Henbane Coven. Nor Grandma, ghost or otherwise. Aunt Shannon and Vanessa's absence was equally odd but made for a much less tense atmosphere. The others might not yet know exactly how this would play out, but there was markedly less chance of a duel between family members breaking out on the stage.

The part I knew would be contentious was that I'd invited members of the other covens, too, with the exception of the Henbanes. The town had a handful of small covens that had little influence, but it wouldn't be fair to exclude them from the process entirely.

When everyone was assembled, I stood at the front and went through the usual introductions, adding that I was glad to see the town recovering so well from the recent attack.

"Sacrifices were made in the process, one of which was the power contained within the ceremonial sceptre," I said. "With the sceptre no longer capable of choosing the new Head Witch, I propose a vote instead, similar to the process by which we typically choose a new coven leader. And we'll hold that vote here and now. Today."

Several people gasped. Most were stunned at the mere audacity of the statement, but a few looked around at the handful of members I'd invited from other covens with marked horror as the prospect sank in that someone other than a Wildwood Coven member—let alone a member of our family—might be next to hold the title. Even Mum's hands clenched so tightly in her lap that her knuckles turned white.

Thanks to Chloe, I'd figured out that I was allowed to do so and that I didn't *have* to mention the open invitation to anyone else in advance of the ceremony. Luckily, nobody kicked up an overt fuss, and I waited for the exclamations and mutters to die out before I continued.

"Before the vote, I have a few more announcements," I said. "The first is that the sceptre will be held within the Head Witch's office regardless of who holds the title. It will play a ceremonial role, no more."

That way, Aunt Shannon couldn't manipulate her way to holding the symbol of our family's magic, and neither could anyone else. That wouldn't stop the wrong person seizing the title itself, but at least the choice would rest upon the people who were actually involved and not an inanimate stick.

I waited for the inevitable gasps to peter out and then moved on. "We'll vote using our wands to conjure a purple light and point at the person who we deem most capable of holding the title of Head Witch."

It was the closest I could come to the process of the original ceremony, and I thought that might help ease the transition for the others. I thought right, and at my command, most people got out their wands.

A cluster of purple lights sprang into existence, glittering throughout the room. When everyone's wand was aglow, I said, "Choose the Head Witch."

The series of sparkling lights blurred then coalesced upon one figure. My mother sat rigidly in her seat, bathed in purple light. Then she rose slowly to her feet.

"The result is clear," I told everyone. "Lady Wildwood is now Head Witch."

Applause rang out, scattered at first, and then enthusiastic. As Mum approached, I stepped back and let her have the stage. I figured she'd already have a speech prepared—since she must have suspected this would happen—but she launched into it with such confidence that I had to wonder if the speech was the same one that she'd originally planned to use when she'd assumed she was going to be chosen to replace Grandma in the first place.

I returned to my seat to listen, and at the end, I applauded along with everyone else.

After the ceremony, we gathered outside in the coven's garden. There was a crisp chill in the air that hadn't been present at the last ceremony more than six months ago, but the breeze was welcome after spending so long inside the stuffy meeting room. I made a beeline for my familiar and found her perched on the fence, with Radcliffe beside her.

"You're finally rid of that giant stick?" Tansy jumped onto my shoulder and gave an affectionate stroke of my ear with the end of her tail. "Excellent."

"Yep." I grinned. "It's over."

"It most definitely isn't." Mum walked over, dismissing an entourage of hangers-on from the ceremony with an impatient hand. "*How* many changes did you make to the rules before you gave up the title, Robin?"

"A few," I admitted. "I did run everything past Chloe first, but we can't let anyone manipulate this new system for their own gain.

"No." She studied me, her lips compressing. "What on earth are you going to do with yourself, then, Robin?"

"Head witch and coven assistant are not the only career paths," I told her. "I already had an offer of a job anyway."

"Courier?"

"No, photographer." I beckoned to Rowan, who was passing, and snagged my camera from her outstretched hand. "For the Sky Hopper championships, for a start, but I can snap some nice shots of the new Head Witch for posterity."

Tansy leaned forward encouragingly. "Go on, Head Witch, smile for the camera."

Mum's scowl deepened. "You've really thought about this? Or did that boyfriend of yours talk you into it?"

"It's what *I* want." I lowered my voice, conscious that people kept stopping to gawk or to listen in on the new Head Witch lecturing her daughter. "Can you please give it a rest? I might not have an official employer yet, but I've been a little busy. Give me a chance."

I'd fallen flat on my face last few times I'd left town, but this was different. I felt like a new person entirely, and not just because I was no longer holding the burden of the Head Witch title either. Mostly, I no longer felt the need to avoid Wildwood Heath for the sake of stubbornness alone or out of a desire to get as far from the coven as humanly possible.

She exhaled in a sigh. "Do as you like, Robin. If you want to work with the coven, you need only ask."

No chance. I'd won the battle, though, and at the very least, she couldn't deny I'd more than done my part to ensure the future of the coven already.

I caught sight of Dad and the family waving at me, and I gladly seized the chance to leave Mum to deal with the gathering coven members who no doubt wanted a piece of the new Head Witch. I definitely wouldn't miss that part of the job, nor the inevitable presence of a certain pair of reporters peering around the hedge.

I'd invited Clarice and Speck myself, with conditions— mostly that they would be the first to print the true version of the story before any of the second-hand rumours currently gracing the tabloid headlines spun even further out of control. Some hadn't even mentioned Linnea, while one had gone out on a limb and claimed Aunt Shannon had been behind the whole thing. If someone didn't get control of the rumour mill and put a definitive story out there, the truth would never be known. And despite my family's usual commitment to secrecy, I wanted the magical world to know just how much my ancestors had sacrificed to defeat the demons and save their home. I didn't want to take the entire credit myself.

Harvey had spotted Clarice and Speck too. As he fell into step with me, he whispered, "Are those reporters supposed to be here?"

"Provided they behave," I replied. "And that Mum doesn't pitch a fit when they tell her they have the right to the first exclusive interview with the new Head Witch."

"Oh, Robin, you didn't. Did you?" Dad had overheard us, and he swept me into a hug when I came to join him and the others. "No more sceptre, then?"

"No more pesky Head Witch title," I agreed. "That's Mum's role—and you can't deny she's more than suited to take my place."

"Definitely can't deny that." He beamed at me. "I'm still proud of my favourite daughter, though."

"I'm technically your only daughter… if you don't count Tansy." My familiar was currently engaged in a teasing chase with Radcliffe, much to the amusement of the two children. "But that wouldn't help you keep the peace with Ramsey."

"He actually offered to babysit for us this weekend while Jess and I go out."

I choked on a laugh. "Seriously?"

I wasn't convinced Ramsey knew exactly what he'd got himself into by offering to babysit two hyperactive shifter kids, but he was standing with Jessica now, watching the squirrels' antics with what might have almost been a smile.

Of course, it wasn't long before he excused himself from the celebrations to get back to work.

Dad and the others, too, had to get back home, and the staring and whispers were getting a bit much for me as well. Harvey and I said our goodbyes to Dad's family and walked through the garden alone. Though heads followed us wherever we went, I knew exactly where we could go to get some privacy. Ducking through a gap in the hedge, I led the way into the maze.

When we reached the fountain at the centre, I stopped. "Weird that this is where it all started, huh?"

"Yeah." His gaze panned over the garden, his smile oddly subdued. "You worked it out with your mother yet? I assume you'll be looking for somewhere outside of Wildwood Heath to live?"

My mouth parted. "No. I haven't had time to think, to be honest."

"Never mind." He held up a hand. "I know you've been busy. I don't want to rush you."

"What—I'm not going to run straight out of town now that I can." I squeezed his other hand. "I have some good reasons to stay, for a start. *Very* good reasons."

This time he smiled for real. "I guess you do. As long as you can handle being around your family. I know you don't want them breathing down your neck all the time."

"I'm always going to have a base here," I told him. "I can guarantee I'll get on better with my family when I'm not under their feet all the time. In other words, not in my childhood bedroom. I'll find another place."

"Or you can move in with me."

My heart skipped a beat. "Not sure you want to drop that one on my mother now. On top of the stunt I pulled at the ceremony, we might shock her into falling into a coma again."

"Do whatever makes you happy, right?"

"You know, I think she might actually be on board with that at last," I said. "It's definitely an improvement."

My heart felt a hundred tons lighter looking around at all the people gathering in the garden, knowing I was no longer responsible for the burden of protecting them or of shoving myself into a role that fit like a pair of odd shoes.

My gaze turned to the open sky, clear despite the cold. Spying a flock of birds flying overhead, I called them to me, and they circled above in a display that looked positively charming and Disney princess-esque. At least until they showered us with feathers.

"Oops." I picked a feather out of Harvey's hair and watched Tansy chase the birds, her fluffy tail gleaming in the sunlight. "I guess my magic needs some fine-tuning after all."

"I think it's just fine." Harvey pulled me into a kiss that made me think of taking flight, the dizzying joy of the ground falling away beneath me.

I was free to look into the future without fear, and whatever path I chose to follow, I'd do it on my own terms.

ABOUT THE AUTHOR

Elle Adams lives in the middle of England, where she spends most of her time reading an ever-growing mountain of books, planning her next adventure, or writing. Elle's books are humorous mysteries with a paranormal twist, packed with magical mayhem.

She also writes urban and contemporary fantasy novels as Emma L. Adams.

Visit http://www.elleadamsauthor.com/ to find out more about Elle's books.